The Gospel of Rot

The Gospel of Rot is one of those novels that sensible writers wish they had written, or perhaps it's one of those novels the world has been hoping *would* be written. Maybe it's one of those novels that has existed, somehow, someway, since the beginning of time. What can I tell you? I'm blown to smithereens with joy about this uncommonly rare and gorgeous work of art. When you read it, your heart and head and belly will glow like Chinese lanterns, and you'll be carried into the very air by Gregory Ariail's exquisite prose and his gemlike observations, and these characters, who will likely be with you for the rest of your life.

—Reginald McKnight,
author of *He Sleeps*

The Gospel of Rot's delight in all manner of fruitfully phantasmagorical decay does indeed verge on the evangelical. It's a heady, keen-eyed evangelism whose fertile language you will be gratefully buttonholed by as it tells you a story, a story of the sometimes immobilizing magic of place, of love, of family, and isolation, and the breaking of that spell that comes only from a blunt-force confrontation with grief. This is a story of revelatory aftermath and the mystery of history, a story as only Gregory Ariail can tell it, a story that will forever change the way you dream.

—Kellie Wells, author of *God, the Moon and Other Megafauna*

The Gospel of Rot

A Novel

GREGORY ARIAIL

MERCER UNIVERSITY PRESS
Macon, Georgia

MUP/ P646

© 2022 by Mercer University Press
Published by Mercer University Press
1501 Mercer University Drive
Macon, Georgia 31207

26 25 24 23 22   5 4 3 2 1

Books published by Mercer University Press are printed on acid-
free paper that meets the requirements of the American National
Standard for Information Sciences—Permanence of Paper for
Printed Library Materials.

Printed and bound in the United States.

This book is set in Adobe Caslon Pro / Luicida Calligraphy display.

Cover/jacket design by Burt&Burt.

ISBN   print   978-0-88146-848-9
ISBN   eBook   978-0-88146-849-6
Cataloging-in-Publication Data is available from the Library of
Congress

For Jessica

MERCER UNIVERSITY PRESS

Endowed by

TOM WATSON BROWN
and
THE WATSON-BROWN FOUNDATION, INC.

Acknowledgments

I am deeply indebted to Jessica Fordham Kidd, without whom this novel would be half itself; Jeremy Packert Burke, for their in-depth comments; Matthew Oglesby's unwavering support and sharp eye; Kellie Wells, for her insight on many chapters; Autumn Fourkiller's thoughtful sensitivity reading of Cherokee elements in the Elodie chapters; Cecilia Piantanida, who helped me realize a number of flaws, especially around the subject of flaccid fingers; the University of Alabama MFA program; my parents for their love and support; Lisa Roney and *Aquifer: The Florida Review Online*, who published an early version of the "Elegy for Dad" chapter; Sara Pirkle for pointing me to MUP; and Marc Jolley, Marsha Luttrell, and Mercer University Press for believing in this project.

Contents

The Gospel of Rot

Last Words

I take out this notebook to transcribe Dad's last words.

"Will you not believe, Amelia?" he said. "The Madonna visited our mountains and I have seen her."

I stayed silent. I couldn't lie to him. I didn't want to accuse him of falsehood, of deliriousness. Rarely had he spoken of the Virgin Mary, so I didn't know how to respond. Tears rose to his eyes.

"Not even for me? You can't believe?"

I shook my head. I almost squeezed his hand but didn't want that to be taken for affirmation.

"I could believe in so much," I said, "but not that. It goes against everything we always thought."

"Then all is lost," he said.

His sweaty head poked out from the pile of dolls that engulfed him, his beloved porcelain and cotton children embracing and nurturing him more fully than I ever could. Their glass eyes accused me of heartlessness.

"If we cannot believe together," he said, "as we have lived together, then a fracture will spread through eternity and we may not meet again."

I kissed his forehead. I traced his white bangs with my fingertips, and pinched them gently, which I knew relaxed him.

"I love you so much," I said.

He nodded and then collapsed into a coughing fit. I wiped the mucus from his chin with a cloth. He was silent for a long time, and then said, "It isn't enough."

That was it. No more words from him to ease the horror of the final, bitter struggle. A shadow passed over our house like a floating mountain.

Elegy for Dad

Along with his dolls, Dad left behind boxes of photographs and a mahogany crucifix on which the Virgin Mary is suspended. Black hair, probably a horse's, flows from the Virgin's scalp and skirts her narrow waist; she has two tiny discs of grey-veined mica for eyes; and her feet are malformed, curving outward like jester shoes. I'd never seen this figurine in my life. I found it in Dad's pocket a few hours after he died. The oddest thing, however, is that—whether a fault of the woodworker, an act of vandalism, or a consequence of one of Dad's devious moods—the Virgin's left breast is missing. The right side has an oval hump, but the left side is flat, smooth, and palely smudged as though rubbed with sandpaper. Along the back of the cross is carved: "To Amelia, from Dad."

We shared many irreverent jokes. Neither of us were orthodox Christians; I'm not sure I was ever a Christian at all. But this figurine, I admit, makes me uneasy.

Dad loved dolls. He kept an extensive collection of them, enough to fill his entire closet. As a child, I could never step foot in that uncanny sanctuary (or, to my mind, mausoleum) without chastisement; although at times, when he was out photographing the mountain landscapes and mountain people—the thing he loved to do above all else—I'd sneak into his closet with a thudding heart and caress their porcelain faces, turn their eyeballs to the left or right, or, when I was especially lonely, embrace them carefully without altering their position.

There were big dolls and little dolls, conventional and quirky ones. A porcelain wizard girl wore a triangular hat adorned with stars; a papier-mâché princess held a hand to her mouth, which was open in surprise; a wooden man in a green cotton cloak, once a marionette, stoppered a flute's holes with wire fingers. Dad photographed them all, but there are no pictures of this Virgin Mary figurine.

Dad was what you might call a shutterbug. He conceived of life as an album of images. His memories, for the most part, were tied to particular photographs he'd taken at one time or another. He entered Kodak contests and lost them. He often wrote Kodak complaining about their overrepresentation of Northern urban photographers and the relative neglect of Southern rural ones in contests; he wrote them about their new products; he wrote them about copyright law. I remember falling asleep to the ring-clack and furious metallic swings and snaps of the typewriter. I can almost hear it now. I keep hearing noises he'd make and mistaking shadows for his presence; I keep glimpsing fragments of him and his belongings—a hand, a shoe, a tripod—appearing and disappearing as through trapdoors. I open my arms to them, but they never remain.

In the 1920s and '30s, each town or hamlet in rural America had its resident photographer (Dad was born in 1889 and I in 1909). These artisans from Hemlock Cove, Olto, Judaculla, and Gallow Hollow frequented Dad's workshop and the Attic Window Darkroom. They'd come with baskets of huckleberries and birch sap candy especially for me. Like Dad, none of them made a splash in the photography world. At best they placed a few pictures in the *Atlanta Journal* or *Audubon Magazine*. But Dad never kept friends long. He'd get into some bitter dispute with them about aesthetics, the superiority of a particular strain of vegetable, or the existence of magic. He had so many of these short-lived artist friends who shared and exchanged photographs with him that it's impossible for me to know which of the thousands of photos he left behind are in fact his. The overwhelming majority are, certainly, but the outliers I can't identify. My eye isn't sharp enough and perhaps his style wasn't distinct enough.

Throughout our lives, Dad and I would venture to the obscurest regions of our property, which was a hundred and twenty acres of oak, creek, and granite dome. He called our home in the cove Amelia's World, because I spent all my time there gardening, walking, and writing while he was off taking pictures. We'd search for lonely, abandoned chimneys from the nineteenth century, the relics of the cabins of Cherokee and frontiersmen, which often tilted dramatically on uneven ground. One can find these all over western North Carolina, hidden in rhododendron coves: creek rocks rising twelve feet high layered with clay chinking and reinforced with rope, hair, and hog's blood. Over time, bees bored into the chinking's hard pottery. Sometimes we'd light a fire in one of these crumbling hearths and smoke would pour out of the holes. Once I tried to take one of the smooth, glittering rocks home, but Dad wouldn't let me because chimney stones, so he said, have magical powers; he told me never to go near a chimney at night because witches use them as way-markers, entering and exiting the otherworld through their flues.

Dad's illness was a painful one. It feels almost irreverent to speak of it. He had bulging sores resembling purple tomatoes, some split open and oozing as if struck by the blight. I dabbed his sores with a cold cloth day and night during the final struggles. His last wish was for me to cover him with his dolls. He tossed and turned, coughing, spitting up fluid and blood; his face jutted out from the top of the porcelain and cotton bodies so that it seemed he wore a grand, puffy Elizabethan dress with ivory lacework. After he lost consciousness, I couldn't stand it anymore and took the dolls away, holding my hand to his bare stomach until the end.

When that fateful moment arrived, I became the embodiment of a silent scream. I thought I saw bright smoke rise from his stomach and condense into a cloud. I still don't know if I was hallucinating, if it was all a dream or if that treasure-chest-sized cloud really did emerge from Dad's body and hover there. I held my gaze to it like I was holding on to the last of Dad's being. *Please stay with me,* I told the cloud. *Just keep part of him living.* But within a few minutes the cloud dimmed. It sizzled, hardened, and sank like a chunk of ice towards his stomach. It looked like a dead thing; all the wonder and brightness had drained away. I snatched the cloud before it pressed down on him and became an appendage to his body; for some reason it seemed obscene to let it touch him. I hauled the cloud out back and pitched it into the pool beneath the cascade. When the cloud hit the water, it blazoned to life one last time. It then became indistinguishable from the granite stones at the pool's bottom. I still don't know which stone it is—if it's even there. I've looked many times for the remnants of that grey-blue cloud. Was it Dad's soul?

After he passed, the world shifted, emptied of color, and I no longer knew who I was or what I wanted. It took a tremendous effort to get out of bed. I thought of a thousand ways I could have nursed Dad better to keep him living one extra day and tormented myself endlessly those first sleepless nights.

I didn't ring the few cousins living in America or the distant relatives in Germany about his illness and death. By now his old friends had mostly passed away; few people ever called or came to visit, and I shooed off the minister who inquired after us the day before he died. I buried Dad myself under the poplar tree. I can't believe it happened just two weeks ago, on October 3. I'd swear it had been two months if the calendar right here didn't contradict me with today's date, October 17. Aside from burying him, I haven't left the house since then. Everything feels tilted. The light streams in differently. Sometimes, in a daze, I hear voices swirling above me, whispering and crying, as though they were part of an invisible tornado siphoning out of the world.

Dad had many sayings: "the best and worst things in life are errors of the stars"; "we're just searching for a lucid interval"; "our knowledge is a journey from ruin to ruin"; "your private conviction shall be universal when the last trumpets blare." I've found myself pondering these cryptic maxims in the days since his death. Over time, we came to share a similar philosophy. We believed travel outside Appalachia, for instance, would not edify the mind. Close observation of oneself and one's immediate surroundings is the key to parting the curtains of mystery, however briefly; sense impressions decay into a precarious reality, and the laws of nature can change at any moment. But we never held our breath awaiting those changes.

Some of his quirks I picked up. We both preferred corncob pipes with bowls cured with apple butter; it made the bright leaf tobacco from our garden taste sweeter and heavier than molasses. I'm smoking an old corncob right now at my writing desk; my hand shakes more than in the past and I pull the smoke with less vigor, but I experience the same relish as in my early adulthood.

Living with Dad was not always easy. Rarely did we get on each other's nerves, but there were times, especially towards the end, when he'd come in needy and sulking, desiring compliments. For sixty-plus years we'd discussed the people and places he photographed and the prints he left lying about the kitchen counter or that he had genuine questions about, which my untrained eye could help him clarify. When his body and spirit began to fray, however, he started leaving photographs in places I'd find when I was alone: on my writing desk, bedspread, and rocking chair. In the garden I once found a Polaroid caught in corn silk. It was a portrait of a woman I'd never met. Her eyes were closed; a horny crust, some kind of skin condition, populated her eyelids. She looked saintly. A band of bright overexposure circled her high forehead like a crown. The next day Dad asked me about it. Was it good or bad? Should he submit it to a magazine?

The first few times he did this, I told him how moving the photographs were. I patted him on the back and flicked him affectionately on his balding pate. But as time passed, it angered me that he wanted me to be his constant praiser and applauder, his confidant in art's triumphs, failures, and transgressions. I wanted nothing more than the communion of easy laughter and the intimacy of long silence. That was how it had always been. It hurt to alter my attitude towards him, to play a role other than daughter. Sometimes I lashed out and said mean things. I regret that.

In the final three years, his liberal spiritual convictions began to wear thin, and I suspected he was becoming secretly zealous in a manner he was embarrassed to admit to me, given our long history of unorthodoxy and light heresies. He'd hide himself away in his workshop reading a copy of the New Testament that he'd picked up at the Baptist church down the road. He dog-eared almost every page of Revelation, highlighting certain passages and redacting others, which was unlike him given how careful we always were with our books; I'd pass him quietly in the living room and say nothing. Once, when he lost his pipe and we couldn't find it anywhere in the house, I heard him mutter, "Madonna, why hast thou forsaken me?" I laughed. I thought it was a joke, but his expression was solemn, even a little pained. In spite of these things, he was my only friend and would've carried the cross for me. An elegy, unlike a eulogy, should be honest in its longing for souls no longer in reach and not shirk the hard truths of a complex life.

On the end table there's a browning, half-eaten peach with Dad's bite mark still intact. I can't throw it away. I think of how often he fretted, especially in the last few years, that all the peach trees in North Carolina were dying. He carefully documented their mutilations after the April freeze. He didn't go exploring the mountains and rivers as far as Asheville anymore but stayed near Amelia's World, beekeeping, making muscadine wine, and worrying over our failing orchard. He often related dreams of worms, molds, and hard white blights like baby teeth infesting the fruit. In his sleep he cried out about plagues and moths. The night before he died, I heard him yell something about "moths burning in the moonlight" and "a scourge of milk."

For some reason I can't help but connect the missing flesh from this half-eaten peach—where Dad's teeth scored as deep as the stone—with the Virgin Mary's missing breast; and I can't help but connect her missing breast to my motherless life. Of all people to have no photographs of, I have none of Mother. Dad took dozens of the goat man who visited the byways of Appalachia once a year in his junk-filled wagon pulled by goats; he has hundreds—literally hundreds—of pictures of purple martins feeding their young from perches in hollowed-out gourds hanging from poles. He even took a few of blurry faces in the woods, possibly the faces of faeries, possibly tricks of light and perspective (not long before his death he burned these eerie photographs). None, however, of Mother. Dad only started documenting the still, silent world after her death.

Mother passed away a few weeks after childbirth (my brother was stillborn) when I was two years old. I was too small to remember her. Like clockwork, once a month, I'd walk into the house to find Dad drinking muscadine wine in the kitchen and crying, almost silently, his shoulders heaving. Few things made me so uncomfortable. It transformed me into his parent. I'd always pretend I didn't see and pass quickly through the room. He never detained me but once. On that particular evening, he spoke about Mother, how, right before she died, bathed in sweat and bright-eyed, she related her favorite memory from their life together. It had to do with an evening in Quedlinburg in northern Germany, the day before she and Dad started their long journey to America. They'd gone walking in the windy autumn hills above the town. They'd held hands; they'd kissed each other's imperfections; they'd talked about what North Carolina might be like as they made for a gap in the trees, where the sun flooded the dim evergreen forest like a bomb's light. In that glade they came across a smooth pink stone shaped exactly like a tongue. Mother picked it up and cleaned it off and put it inside her mouth for a moment. It proved to be the same size as her tongue. She threw it away but wished she'd kept it. It was such a rare little stone. Dad had no memory of the day she spoke of and that bothered him, made him worry he'd taken her for granted.

Dad, you were good to me. You were strong and gentle and careful as a mother. I'm a seventy-one-year-old woman now. It's a testament to you that I have no fear of the darkness or the light. Every square inch of this house is haunted by your presence, but I can't find you. As I turn this effigy of the Virgin Mary back and forth under candlelight, I want to glean more details, to see her mica eyes flash at me. I know that this object is some kind of provocation from you; a sign that I should rethink my life, my past and future, even at this late stage. It makes me wonder what other secrets you kept from me in that closet of dolls, which did not replace me, exactly, but acted as a surrogate for something I can't understand. What perversions, mean hates, and desires so naive and saccharine as to be almost scandalous did you hide from me? And where should I go now? What should I do? If I crack open the Virgin's wooden skull, will there be a ball of mica inside it, a mineral brain not so different from my own? Will a thought rise from it like smoke and hover there like the cloud that came from your body?

The sky is the dark orange of persimmon beer as I finish this elegy. Orion, the hunter constellation, sparkles along the trees but Sirius has yet to appear. Perhaps I have twenty more years left, and I'll die at ninety-one, just like you. But with this inexplicable figurine in my hand, what tables should I turn to honor, spite, or abandon you? Is the Virgin a key to open the kingdom within?

Details in the Apples

I've come up with a plan to while away the desiccated, vacant days without Dad, without his steady loves, worries, impositions, and complaints. Each day, I'll choose a photograph from the folders of his landscapes and visit whatever location speaks to me. I'll leave off farming and foraging (fortunately, I have enough canned fruit and pickled vegetables to last me another twenty years if need be) and venture out into the mountains he came to know so intimately over the years. Each evening, I'll come home and write down my adventures. I haven't kept a journal in years and it'll be refreshing to do so again, however loosely.

Somehow Dad's death, now that the period of paralysis is over, has released me from my self-imposed isolation; I chose to stay put in Amelia's World partly from sorrow and shame and partly from habit and sheer stubbornness. Now it's time to leave at last. I'm at loose ends in this painfully empty house with nothing to do but take care of myself. I must put aside Dad's last words, telling me my love wasn't enough, and try to honor and remember him in a different way. Today isn't the day to document the reasons why, after age eighteen, I never left the property. That's, as they say, a story for stormy weather, not a seductive, cool, windy day like this. Later on, I'll tell why I chose to work the fields, forage, and smoke my corncob pipe and let Dad do the outside errands: the driving to market and the churchgoing just to show the neighbors we weren't total miscreants.

So, after shuffling through a batch of photographs like a deck of tarot cards, I selected a green-tinted one of Oldcastle Quarry, the only place to extract rubies, mica, granite, and coal from a single location on earth. That's where I decided to go; but, as it happened, I didn't make it.

My soul beat with blood when I stepped off the property after all those years. As I pushed my bike onto the asphalt, I felt half certain I'd have a heart attack and die on the spot. I often imagined that Amelia's World lay on a lonely branch of the world tree, or that our property was enclosed in an ethereal, needle-sharp webbing that I couldn't cross without causing serious damage to my organs. But I took those momentous steps and came through unharmed, back in the outer world after so long. I did a little twirl, got dizzy, and had to pause for a second. I pictured myself as a sailor on the cusp of a great expedition, having just unmoored my ship from the shore.

As I mounted my bike unsteadily, I began to tear up with relief at the sudden collapse of my superstitions and a way of life I'd never live again. What would Hemlock Cove be like now? For most people in North Carolina and the wider world, I've heard that everything's changed, but for me little has changed and it feels like it should still be 1926. While I've glimpsed newfangled cars swerving through the trees, on the whole Hemlock Cove has stayed so insulated, and so few new houses have been built, that Dad always said that to an outsider the experience of driving down our road would be eerie, since there are hardly any indications of the late twentieth century.

With the Virgin Mary tucked in my jeans pocket, I rode towards Oldcastle Quarry. There was something new in the air; something more than wonder, pleasure, and fear at finally leaving home. I sensed it as I wobbled down the road: a subtle new bend to the trees, a blown glass aspect to the sky, shadows awakening between the landscape and my soul. It was strange that this newness should coincide with Dad's passing, as if his death had unlocked a fresh set of natural laws. For some time now, the cries and whispers in the sky, which were certainly just the echoes of my despair, had subsided. Everything was silent. I'd expected to be overwhelmed by a litany of half-forgotten sounds: neighbors' chatter, children playing, horses neighing, and the like.

No automobiles passed by flinging gravel into my face, as happened so often when I was a girl and rode my rose-colored bicycle down this once unpaved road, either to the Hemlock Cove Schoolhouse, which I attended until I was sixteen, or to the Chattooga River, where I'd swim and slide down the smooth waterfalls with other children (they rarely paid much attention to me, but I didn't really mind them forgetting about me when we played hide-and-seek).

I rode three miles to the southeast, past the brush arbor and the horse pasture, until my calf muscles felt strained and my lungs spent. I needed to take a break before continuing on to Oldcastle Quarry. The old orchard on the wayside called to my heart to stop by for a visit: the last time I'd seen it had been one May day long ago when the trees were bloated with white petals.

I leaned my bike against a honey locust tree, careful to avoid its thorns, and stepped over a collapsed section of barbed-wire fence. I leapt over a gully and proceeded up the gradual grassy hill to the thermal belt ideal for apple growing. The weeds were littered with fragments of broken crockery jugs and canning jars. The sun poured glass through the apple trees aligned in snug, even rows; they were contorted and heavily shagged with lichen. The October wind moved the leaves and sent apples showering to the earth, forming big piles beneath the branches. Some errant apples rolled to my feet and collapsed into mush when they touched my shoe.

I looked around for Endicott the orchardist, forgetting that he'd been dead for more than thirty years. I reckoned there must be another orchardist on the premises who could explain this curiosity to me: why the apples had become so delicate they fell apart of their own accord and why they gathered in huge mounds. There were too many apple trees well trimmed and tended for the orchard to have gone to seed; there must be a keeper somewhere. Yet his or her refusal to shovel away and compost these large piles of apples, rising like miniature mountain ranges beneath the trees and reaching as high as my breasts, suggested the opposite case—that the orchard was derelict. How many years had it taken to amass that much apple mush: a decade or more?

I navigated the labyrinthine mounds, passing different varieties of apple trees, all with lovely names—Red June, Brown Snout, Blacktwig, Cullasaga, Edward's Winter, Fallawater, Foxwhelp, Ooten, Smokehouse, Wolf River. These names were printed on fading placards nailed to the trunks. Endicott the orchardist, with his severe white mustache and blue eyes, explained many things to me about the orchard life when I was a girl: apple varieties, diseases and pests, the grafting process. But from his long-winded speeches I only remember his theory of apple cider, how the best cider is a combination of three different kinds of apples—one sweet, one tart, and one fragrant. The last time I saw him, he bragged good-naturedly that his apples were not just a local fetish anymore but were shipped as far as Cuba, Puerto Rico, Liverpool, and Hamburg.

While I searched an outstretched branch for a pristine fruit to pluck, I noticed something odd. I took a magnifying glass from my satchel, bent down, and held it to the pile.

What should have been anonymous heaps of apple mush revealed themselves to be, under the optical sharpness of my magnifying glass, miniature human bodies. Each one no longer than a fingernail. All these miniature human bodies were stark naked. There were, just in this one pile, probably tens of thousands of bodies; the brown bodies, the color of apple meat exposed to the air, formed by far the highest percentage. They heaved up from the grass four feet or more—what looked like tiny men, women, and children with facial features far too small to discern with any preciseness. White bodies formed a delicate layer, a patina, on the ridge of the pile, resembling a dusting of snow; some of the white bodies, no bigger than carpenter ants, slipped down a chute in the mounds like half-formed cascades. The sight shook and bewildered me.

"Been awhile," the orchardist said, interrupting my observations.

I looked up at a tree, and there was his face, old Endicott Hoyt's face, outlined in the leaves and apples; curves in the leaves formed the orchardist's head and a clump of lichen a minty green mustache. Two chips of blue sky between the leaves created the impression of eyes.

The world has indeed changed, I thought, caressing the Virgin Mary in my pocket, tremblingly tracing her body's outline.

"It has *indeed*," the tree face said.

I backed away a little. This wasn't totally unexpected. I'd always kept my mind receptive to tears in the fabric of reason and experience, to a time when the world, like a glass onion, would crack, or its smeared surface become suddenly clear, allowing one to glimpse layer upon layer of truths receding to the core. What unsettled me most was that this great change dovetailed with Dad's death and my departure from the property. What other secrets had Dad kept from me? How long had things been so different? Had he been protecting me from an unstable reality, a world in the wind? I couldn't help but doubt my sanity for a moment, but no—I was secure in myself. My fear was soft and murmuring, the kind one feels during a light fever or after an unpleasant dream.

"Hello there," I said, taking careful steps backwards and edging towards my bicycle.

"See you later," I declared, regaining my hermit's confidence. "Sorry to bother you, I've got a busy day ahead—just haven't been here in years and thought I'd stop by. Wasn't right of me."

"Speak *inside*," the orchardist said, his leaf mouth opening and closing. "So I can hear you."

"Inside what?" I thought.

"There you go. I can hear you loud and clear. Now we can have a proper conversation."

"Is she there, too—Lully, your wife?" I thought hesitantly, not sure whether I'd got the name right. I had known the pair fairly well, but not overly, merely as neighbors a few miles apart know each other.

Wind lifted the leaves. A tight-knuckled apple fell precipitously and exploded on the heap.

"I knew you at once," he said. "Your hair is longer, whiter, frizzier. But your posture is the same, very straight-backed, with the same muscular forearms as when you were a girl."

Silence intervened. I didn't like when people talked about my appearance, but I was aware of my good posture and didn't need reminding. I thought of Lully, the orchardist's wife, with her own waist-length white hair. She'd cored, peeled, and quartered apples, drying them on wire screens and stringing them on thread until they turned brown. She'd make apple butter in a brass kettle, stirring with a cypress stick and adding molasses, lemon, and cinnamon. I saw her perform this ritual one October. I considered her the apple wizard. Together, Lully and Endicott would harvest thousands of bushels a year. It's amazing to think there are still ten or eleven crocks of their apple butter in my cellar.

"I see and hear your thoughts," the orchardist said. "They give me pain. They make me feel a great loss."

I tried to remember when Lully died, to remember details of her funeral, which I'd heard of but not attended. Without a doubt I would've been there if it hadn't occurred after my decision to quit the busy fray of desire and reap the simpler pleasures of life.

"1946. That's when the diabetes took her. What year is it now?"

"1980," I thought.

The lichen-mustache fluttered above the orchardist's lip. The gaps between the leaves that formed his blue eyes widened and narrowed in the breeze.

"I see your father has passed, too. I can remember his strange patois, mountain dialect with a German inflection. Not even during the War did anyone question him. That's saying something. Y'all were one of us; if someone said otherwise, well, good luck to them. The last year I remember living—1949? '50?" He was silent for a moment. His thoughts changed tack. "Am I with Lully and your father or apart from them? I woke up when you entered the orchard. But before that…" His words veered again. "I hope y'all were on good terms at the end. You and your father, I mean. I teased her, you know. My wife. Life was hard so I liked to make a joke of it. I played practical jokes a lot—you might remember. I played one on Lully the day before she died. That blunder haunted me the three or four years I survived her—if I survived her?"

His blue-sky eyes closed. A branch halfway down the trunk lifted a few inches, as if to touch his face, but couldn't make the entire journey. It fell back down, shuddering and raining lichen flakes.

"As I was saying, in August 1946, Lully sat in the roadside woods in her favorite oak chair, the one I made. Her feet and legs were swollen and black and purple as though injected with venom—that was the diabetes' doing. A terrible disease. It burnt away the joy, all the ease, that affliction. In the morning I'd carried her out to that chair underneath the trees and laid a cloth down at her feet so that she wouldn't get them dirty. Well, I wanted to cheer her up, you know.

"The night before, by lantern light, I'd taken one of the scarecrows from the cornfield and tied a rope to its pitchfork spine and hoisted it into the treetop. As my love—sharp, generous, brilliant Lully, who to this day I can't believe said yes—well, as she sat there gazing out at the newly paved road, totally absented, dwelling, I imagine, on her pain and on childhood memories, I lowered the scarecrow bit by bit, trying to keep the branch from creaking or shaved bark from pattering down upon her. I bit my knuckles. The scarecrow was an inch above her head when she finally noticed the sackcloth face, the marker-drawn black eyes, the mouth I'd taped so hay wouldn't spill out. She screamed one piercing note and her eyes clouded over. I jumped out from the azalea bush with a goofy grin on my face, but she comprehended nothing but her own terror.

"That was the day before she died. It took her three hours to regain the power of speech. And she wouldn't look at me. Usually a woman to laugh uproariously, on that last night she never met my eyes."

"Don't torture yourself," I said hesitantly. "It's not worth it. Dad would say that was just an error of the stars."

"Speak *inside!*" the orchardist resumed testily—this time, however, from a different direction. I angled myself this way and that but couldn't locate his face in the treetop anymore. "Come on over to the Ooten tree…that's to your right! Your right, not left! That's the Red June…a few steps farther, yes, yes…the one with the giant fruits with greenish-yellow skin, bark looks like a hog's face squashed flat. It's labeled too, right here, but don't *touch*!"

I stood before another apple heap, whose diminutive summits curved like ancient mountains. This one was quite runny, a mix of peels and applesauce when looked at without using my magnifying glass—which I hesitated to do again, although I still felt intensely curious about the miniature bodies I'd seen before.

"It's vague, your speaking," the orchardist said, "but I can hear it in whispers and starts as though from a cellar with the door ajar." He paused, thoughtfully. "You've noticed the bodies in the apple piles; that's keen of you. What are they, you say? Why have many years' worth of apples gathered beneath the trees to rot? On the one hand—now bear with me, because I only half understand this myself—well, they seem to be first folk, the Mississippians, the Cherokee, ten thousand years of the dead, and only recently the Spanish, English, Scots-Irish, Germans, the frontiersmen and mountaineers: the whites dribbles of snow on a foundation nearly as deep as the mountains themselves. From a distance the mounds just look like small models of mountains made of apples. But up close, you see that the apples are, in fact, legions of the dead. Nowadays things can be two things at once; formerly, if I remember rightly, that wasn't the case."

I thought about the great depths of Appalachian history, how me and Dad and our little lives had been just the tip of the iceberg, and below that eons of other people, animals, and plants. I nearly lost my balance. It then occurred to me that perhaps a tiny version of Dad lay somewhere in the heaps, but finding him would take months, perhaps years, with those hundreds of millions of corpses. And if I wanted to visit his real remains, they were still fresh under the poplar tree.

"No more thoughts of Daddy today," the orchardist said. "It's distressing you. He was an interesting man—leave it at that. Let me help you. Come, look at the Ooten tree."

I lifted my eyes to the tree's crown. And there the orchardist's face appeared again. This time a grey-white, serrated, and horizontal leaf formed his mustache; the wrinkles in his face were indicated by cobwebs; his eyes, instead of chips of daylight, were giant blue apples.

"Don't look at me, that won't do any good. Look right in front of you at the bark. See—it's like a hog's face squashed flat. Within that face, where a nostril would be, there's a chink—a keyhole. Maybe you have a key to unlock it? I'd wager so by the look of that bunched-up pocket. I'm a messenger. I don't think I chose to come to life by myself. Another managed it somehow."

I withdrew the mahogany Virgin Mary from my pocket.

The Ooten bark did seem to contain, as the orchardist said, a swinish face within it; and indeed, there was a chink where the hog's nostril would be that invited the Virgin Mary figurine. Her head, even with its mane of black horsehair, fit perfectly into the tree; her single breast, like an oiled bit, slid into the groove smoothly as water. I turned her and a hidden bolt clicked and released in the heartwood. The tree itself didn't open as I expected. No staircase spiraled down into the earth.

"What happens now?" I thought, looking up to the orchardist. His face was no longer discernible in the leaves. I called his name. I called again. I searched the apple heaps and wound between the rows of trees calling "hello?" and "where'd you go?" and "Endicott?" But he never answered.

Not knowing what to do, and feeling so abandoned and confused I wanted to cry, I returned to the Ooten tree. Luckily the Virgin figurine was still there, wedged to her buttocks in the trunk. I twisted her back to the left and she yielded.

Suddenly the world grew dimmer as though a sheet had been thrown over the sun. The mother star was still high in the cloudless sky, yet it cast a dusky silver light. Was it just my imagination? Had the day passed more quickly than I'd thought?

As I examined the Virgin in my hand, a little worried that the tree had injured her, I realized that something was in fact different about her eyes. They were now wooden rather than mineral and sparkling; deep-set rather than rotund. The two discs of grey-veined mica that had previously inhabited her sockets were missing, eaten by the tree. I peered into the keyhole and scratched around the heartwood with my pinky but couldn't exhume her eyes. Pensive and worn out, I got back on my bicycle and rode home rather than continuing on to Oldcastle Quarry. I'll do that tomorrow. Tonight I need to rest my sore calves and ease my spinning brain.

The Mica Children

It's no surprise that my dreams last night were troubled. In one of them I crawled through a mineshaft and came out upon those mountains of preserved bodies, but instead of being miniature, they rose thousands of feet into the air. I searched a slope's base for a long time before finding an adequate route up the mountain. In one place the bodies had folded into each other to form stairs like the horizontal impressions of an ancient waterfall. They varied in pigmentation, length and color of hair, and bone structure, but none of them had eyes—rather, screwed into the two sockets were whorled, cream-colored snail shells. Every face contained this anatomical curiosity. There were millions of bodies and millions of snail shells sunk perfectly into the eye sockets. Once, somewhere near the summit, my foot got stuck in a stratum of gunk; and when I sat down on a stomach to scrape it away (the stomach's flesh was dry and cracked like pottery exposed to the sun), the gunk contained the green fabric of leaves and bones so tiny you'd think they came from fruit flies.

When I awoke, I couldn't stop shaking. I got up and called my distant cousin, Tempie Astor. I hardly ever use the phone; I was clumsy with the dial wheel but eventually got the number right. Tempie didn't answer, however. She was the type to always answer the phone, out of breath from running across the living room but always in time to scoop up the receiver. When her end stopped ringing, something happened: a boy's voice floated through a cloud of static, singing the same verse over and over as if practicing for choir: "not see, but sing, not see, but sing, not see, but sing." I tried to interrupt and ask the boy who he was but got no reply.

I worried over this for a while. Had another phone line crossed over with my own? (I understand little of such things). I tried to think of another person to call. The closest neighbors were the Hillipses, and after searching the kitchen for the address book, I found their number. No one answered at their house either. This time, static arose, and then a little girl's voice penetrated the white noise. She sang a verse twice: "each one a true, each one a true." Then the static resurfaced.

I would have turned on the television, but Dad and I didn't believe in them. We never owned one and I never saw one myself, only heard about them from visitors (we went to the movies once after the Great War, in 1919 I believe, to see *Ivanhoe* with King Baggot; the event never repeated itself).

No matter which way I turned the dial of the radio, it sounded like snakes having a hissing contest. I thought I might hear something about a mass blackout, a message from President Carter, or a devastating storm sweeping across America. But nothing except snakes hissing.

I opened the screen door and walked outside, across a mat of tulip poplar leaves that, seemingly overnight, had turned yellow and tooth-decay brown and fallen. I crossed the field and entered Dad's workshop and stood over his table. I picked up the photo of Oldcastle Quarry, whose sheer cliff face curved like a projection screen.

I dropped the photograph on the table and shouldered my satchel, deciding that stewing here over these insoluble questions and anxieties would do no good. I must buck up and pick up where I left off; chance had dropped its coin on the quarry. On the way, I'd call on a couple neighbors to see if they could explain the cove's emptiness.

My body was so sore from my exertions yesterday that I could hardly pump the pedals of my bike at first. I managed to steer the bicycle masterfully and impressed myself. I was glad to see this old body function so well, but it's no surprise, really, given that I've always exerted myself in the garden and hardly ever eaten a scrap of meat. I hadn't driven a car in fifty years, and balked at the thought of it, so I wasn't upset that Dad sold the old Ford six months before his passing, knowing that I preferred old-fashioned exercise to modern speed and comfort.

The puddles in the Hillipses' gravel driveway splashed my jeans. My shoes, when I dismounted, sank into the leaves and water flooded them. I cursed as I climbed the porch steps and knocked on the front door. No one answered. I knocked louder and louder until my knuckles bruised. I went around back to the horse pasture. The black and white burned cliff of Devil's Lozenge rose gigantically behind the woods, with dwarf shrubs dotting the occasional chip or exfoliation patch in the granite. No sounds broke the silence; no children ran about or yelled from the tops of the hemlocks. I looked for the horses; they weren't in the fields or in the stable and I heard no neighing.

I wouldn't exactly mind if most people in the area had gone away for some unexplained reason, but I wasn't comfortable with the prospect. It would beg too many questions. How ironic that after so long, when I finally leave my house, and the worst phase of grief is over, the entire world has become a kind of hermitage. A small part of me wanted to see people again.

I got back on my bike. The sun shined more dimly than ever before at this time of year, as though tinted glass were held in front of it. I stopped by the old grouch Alvert Hastie's trailer, knocked and called his name (he'd visited our house a couple times). I held my ear to the door for a while. Nothing—no vociferous coughs, no cigarette smoke leaking from cracks. I kept glancing suspiciously at the trees in his yard, expecting to see Alvert's face appear in the branches at any moment.

I remounted my bike and soon came to the orchard. Part of me was tempted to go find Endicott, but I doubted he was in the trees anymore, and even if he was, he hadn't been much help yesterday.

So I carried on and approached the point where the bottomlands end and the mountains rise again. I pumped up the first hill without much problem; on the second upward slope I had to walk alongside my bike. How tiring! It almost made me forget the cove's emptiness. Soon enough I passed from asphalt to dirt and covered the two-odd miles from the orchard to the quarry. Not a soul who isn't from here, and hasn't lived in this region for a long time, would know where Oldcastle Quarry is on Grimshawe Road. It hides behind a steep tunnel of rhododendron leaves and is canopied further by giant tulip poplars. It's a rock city no one would suspect from the road. There's no sign for the quarry, not anymore. It's an abandoned place.

Exertion up a steep trail at altitude—even at 3,000 feet, trust me—can be difficult for an average person half my age. I managed the hundred yards without too much trouble, stopping a couple times with my arms akimbo and sucking in the wet air leaking from the mine shafts, caverns, and grottos. And soon a minor vista met my gaze. The terraced, dynamited remnants of a mountain's heart, excavated and ravaged. It was like a high druidic monument dangling with boulders. Here one had to be careful, to listen for the patter of gravel, the growl of stone; a small but deadly avalanche could occur at any moment. In fact, seven men had died here in an accident long ago.

As my eyes adjusted to the dim landscape, the uniqueness of this conglomerate quarry-mine struck my curiosity more forcefully than it had fifty-odd years ago. The amphitheater was naturally divided into three parts with three different types of rocks composing the formation, folding outward like a triptych. The left column was loose muddy emery, containing corundum and rubies; the center column was a grey and sparkling interlayer of granite and silver mica; the right column was coal with a reptilian submetallic luster. Here igneous and sedimentary rocks stood shoulder to shoulder, mixed with an array of common and precious minerals (the latter have mostly been pillaged, but the attuned eye can still find them). Scattered about were caves and mine shafts I dared not enter. A boulder sat precariously atop a nearby fissure.

Something attracted my attention. The sunlight fanning out from the east caught a broken sheet of mica and poured light into creases on its surface.

I picked it up and examined it closely. Inside the mica's mirror were the images of two children, both sitting on chairs. For a half-second I wondered if they were my reflection, if I'd grown two children's heads like a Hydra, but I touched my face and felt nothing except the old solitary head with wrinkles and bags under the eyes. I turned this way and that, wondering if the children were standing beside me or somewhere nearby. Seeing no one, I looked at the mica again. The girl's chair was large and misshapen; undoubtedly her mother, with a bedsheet thrown over her body to conceal her, acted as the seat for the child. I could just make out the impression of an arm beneath the cloth. The girl had curly hair, rosy cheeks, and wore a white dress and black boots. The boy was perhaps a year older and sat by himself on a chair patterned with azalea cups. His hair was combed to the side, his lips were thick with the Cupid's bow dipping dramatically, and an ear stuck out horizontally. The images reminded me of daguerreotypes, with shades of mercury vapor, gold chloride, and silvered copper. They were like fossils imprinted in a glittering silver frame.

Then came the eerie chants I'd heard earlier through telephone static: "Not see, but sing, not see, but sing; each one a true, each one a true." Even though the children in the mica were too young to sing such high treble notes—they were no older than three—their little mouths moved ever so slightly.

The melodies came from within the mica; the thin sheet vibrated in my hand.

The girl's tiny mouth closed after singing the word "true." A hissing ensued.

"Can you hear me?" I asked the children.

The boy's ethereal voice rang out clear: "the Baptist, Judas, Sabbatai Zevi, each one a true"; and then the girl's voice added like bells ringing: "I came in their name."

"Now don't be cryptic," I scolded. "You both have very beautiful voices, so thank you for that performance. What I need is help. Do you know Emil Hollwede—my dad? I know that's crazy to ask, but no more crazy than y'all two. Or Endicott the orchardist? Is he in there with you, moping around and reading minds even when no one gives him permission? Tell Endicott I want someone to explain what's going on because Dad never mentioned a single damn thing about a mass exodus or the end of times. Even the sun is different. That's weighing on me."

I gave the children the best evil eye I could, but I also feared they'd go away if I grew too harsh. It was a relief to have human beings to look at even if the conversation was going nowhere. In my fancy the pair were inhabitants of this place before it was gutted for profit; perhaps they died young, like so many children in this region did, and haunted the quarry.

The mouths opened and closed again, but no musical words floated from the silver surface. Then, as if the sounds and movements were not properly synchronized, they began again, this time in chorus: "wrong," they sang, their heads tilting from side to side, "even the elect are deceived, from one wind a door from afar, no war." The boy sang a verse alone: "heaven and earth beyond my voice." And then the girl: "I say to you—don't look." The boy sang: "The trinity, to have no root: Nazareth, Golgotha, Carolina." And the girl: "The trinity, to have no root: Rome, Bethlehem, Judaculla." And together: "Inner light, outer light, inner light, outer light."

The children's hymns ended and the hissing resumed. They stared at me with smiles in their eyes. Their words rang obscurely in my mind, with a power behind the obscurity, like parables without a key. My rational mind didn't follow anything about this string of Christian nonsense.

"I hate to be mean, but are you two off your rockers? Are you all there? Do you understand me?"

I said the same sentences inside my head, just in case they, like the orchardist, could only perceive thoughts. This produced the same disappointing result. I started to pace. Suddenly a small avalanche sent plumes of dust across the coal formation to my right. I jumped impulsively and made a tight fist. The plume migrated and settled.

When I opened my hand again, the mica children had been crushed into grains of sparkling sand. My chest heaved and my lips trembled. I felt like I'd lost something precious after just finding it. My impulse was to try to piece together the grains, spending weeks or months reconstructing the two children, even if they spoke nothing but gibberish. They would've been decent companions, a bit frustrating with all the singing and hissing, but ones I could take home and keep at my bedside or, better, on the mantel with my bedroom door closed so I could get some sleep at night. Then the pointlessness of that task hit home; the children were gone for good. I poured the handful of dust into my left pocket. In my right the Virgin Mary angled woodenly against my thigh.

For an hour or more I searched the rocks for other mica sheets with children inside but had no luck. I was sick of being alone in that desolate heap of ruins. I called out to Dad. Because why not? Was he hidden, like Endicott, somewhere in these mountains he loved? It made me want to explore

Hemlock Cove all the more. Maybe the Virgin is a key to find his soul or a version of him that's been sucked into the land's veins and reformed. Maybe everyone that's gone has been translated into the earth. But only my echoes answered me in that quarry, so I made my way home.

On the way back, I could have sworn a tiny figure moved along the crest of Devil's Lozenge, only to disappear. I stopped my bike. I heard a distant cry. Was it "help," "hello," "hell," or just another echo of my longing? Once again I called out, and once again received no reply.

Something's accruing. The sun has changed in a way that scares me; it seemed, last time I glimpsed it, to contain a shape in its dim golden orb resembling a stick figure. The orchardist and the mica children were far less alarming to me than this sun, which appears like a cooler star from another solar system.

The Evening Door

In the middle of the night, I woke up in the throes of vertigo, my head spinning and throbbing, my stomach heaving acid into my throat whenever I changed positions. I gripped my quilt with sweaty hands.

Now it's late afternoon. The tobacco flowing through my system doesn't cure the hangover, but it steadies my nerves, adds some weight to my being, which wild, barbed spirals were shredding to bits. I haven't left home all day or selected a new photograph, a fresh location to explore, from Dad's folders. I need to dwell on something other than him, other than my love that wasn't enough. The outside world, with its Endicotts and mica children, can wait. I've made a fire with oak, ash, and applewood logs; the fireplace produces an incense, and the cheeks of the two cornhusk dolls on the kitchen shelf flicker with light. A steady rain falls on the roof. Scurrying leaves click against the window and thunder rumbles distantly, regularly, like a giant's footsteps.

In times of illness, I can't think linearly, but images from the past—and especially Elodie's face—take on a life of their own. Memories that I've long forgotten or repressed break into the field of consciousness. Last night her face kept lowering towards my own like a scarecrow on a rope that then jerked away. Vertigo—that's what it was like in some ways back then when I fell in love with Elodie. Unlike this present, uncharted phase of my history, the chaos of the mid-1920s, the years that rocked my soul and made me the person I am today, had an eye amid the storm.

Elodie was that eye, for one little year (it's hard to believe only that much). She was ten years older than me and married to the prosperous owner of a grocery store and filling station.

To most people's eyes, we were the best of friends; few knew why our friendship suddenly broke off and why, afterwards, my personality and habits altered so dramatically that I became known as the hermit of Hemlock Cove.

It was June 1926. I'd recently finished my education at the old one-room Hemlock Cove Schoolhouse. As a graduation present, the schoolmistress gave me a beautiful pine writing table with a dove-tailed drawer and tapered legs—the one I'm writing on now, in fact, which, minus a few scuffs, is the same as it was then. So, yes, I was helping a young pupil with her arithmetic as a favor to the much pressed-upon schoolmistress when a car crunched up the gravel drive, one of those early edition Model Ts. Through the open window I glimpsed, in the driver's seat, a fascinating face—unshapely but strong in effect, giving the woman's profile a curious magic.

Farther up the gravel drive lay a graveyard. The schoolhouse had once been a frontier Baptist church; its graveyard, as far as I knew, was derelict—no fresh graves had been dug during my lifetime—and few people drove up that way (though we children often played there during lunch hour). The schoolmistress told me to pause a moment and hurry after the car and wave the driver down, so that she might park down here and not get stuck in the deep, awkward ruts up ahead.

I ran after the car, waving frantically, my dress soaked with sweat by the time the woman stopped, contorting her peach-fuzz-covered face to view me and receive my message.

"What is it?" she said a little curtly. "This isn't private property."

"No, ma'am, that isn't it," I said, huffing, catching my breath. "I'm sorry to make you stop and all, but I was sent to tell you how bad the road gets up above here. There are lots of ruts and gullies."

She gave me a sharp look. Her blue eyes had golden, wavering, delicate threads that accentuated the blue. Her expression relaxed. She smoothed down her short black hair.

"Well, get in," she said.

It wasn't like me to get in a stranger's vehicle, but I didn't hesitate to open the passenger door and jump into the seat beside her. I noticed dried goldenrod and mugwort in the empty space on the black leather seat between us, tied together with red string and so perfect they must have been bought at a store. The car smelled like a forest, yet also of gasoline and the tonic she used in her hair.

"Tell me where the ruts are and we'll avoid them, okay? I'm from around here, you know, so I can handle it." She hesitated a moment. "Are you a student at the school?"

"I used to be. I'm just helping out since I live down the road."

"In Hemlock Cove?"

"Yes," I said, as the car dipped suddenly, its undercarriage scraping a rock and then bouncing upwards.

"Well damn," she said. "Not doing your job."

We both laughed. After navigating a few more bumps and hollows, she parked the car by a hemlock stand. As she got out, I examined her clothing. She wore a white collared shirt with the sleeves rolled up past her elbow, cream-colored breeches, striped socks, and grey canvas shoes with squat heels. I was mesmerized by her strange outfit. I felt like a dinosaur, waddling after her in my wide checkered dress that could've been worn without much embarrassment in the 1800s.

"And where're you from?" I called after her as we climbed the uneven steps to the graveyard. "Atlanta?"

"Oh goodness no," she said. "I told you I'm from around here—Attic Window! Just up the road." As we crested the hill, and came among granite headstones, she added: "I'm Elodie."

"Amelia," I said.

"We've got that out of the way. Now come over here and help me find a name—Irona Bumrucker. Can't forget that, hm?"

"Who is she?" I asked, bending down and reading a weathered, nearly illegible name in low relief.

"My Granma. Never seen her grave before. Can you believe it? Getting older makes you sentimental, I guess."

We wandered about for a few minutes, weaving in and out of shadow, searching for Irona's name.

"Ah, here it is," she said. I was a little upset she'd found it first.

"And look," she added as I entered the sunlight. "Three granddaddy longlegs mating; is that what they're doing?"

I bent down. "I suppose it is," I said.

On the gravestone, covering the C and K in Bumrucker, three granddaddy longlegs sat atop one another, like crowder peas with numerous spindly legs. They were motionless. The only movement came from a thin black leg, seemingly one of the harvestmen's, twitching a couple inches away from the group as though it were amputated, just above the I and the R in Irona.

"Do they usually mate in threes?"

"I don't know," I said. "I've never seen that before."

I counted the legs as best I could. "Twenty-three legs."

"And why is that leg detached? The twitching one. Did they have a fight?"

"Maybe."

She bent down to the tombstone and wiped some dirt from the letters. Her energy tightened its rope around my heart, drawing me towards her.

"I never met Granma—only recently I found her scrapbook in an old safe my mother left me. I just opened it for the first time yesterday. I was bored. And I learned her name for the first time, too. It's strange. I like to think of the past, or certain strands of the past, but others are a darkness to me."

She ran her slim fingers over the cut granite. She touched the amputated, twitching leg with her fingertip and traced circles around the three grandaddy longlegs mating motionlessly in the sunlight.

"Will you come visit me in Attic Window?" She said it offhandedly, but with the slightest tremor. She looked at me steadily and I blushed.

"When?"

"Tomorrow. At lunch? I'll come get you—no, no, I'll do that, I insist—don't speak of walking. That car's as good as my own, you know, so it's no problem. Now let's drive you back down to the school."

The next day we stood in my living room, next to the fireplace on whose mantel many dolls sat or lolled, some with dainty legs crossed, some twined together in innocent embrace. A bookshelf, half-stocked with volumes, rose to our right. Dad, in his starched shirt and checkered tie, stood with impeccable posture.

"So you are the friend Amelia told me about," he said in his slow, precise English. "Elodie McWaters? Oh, I've heard of you, yes. I met your mother ten years ago—the year of the flood."

"Good day," Elodie said, shaking his hand heartily. "So the McWaters are known down here in Hemlock Cove? I'm glad you didn't call me by my husband's name—I hate that sort of thing, though I get endless grief about it from my family." She cocked her head slightly. "I'm sure I've seen you before—the photographer and handyman! Ah, I thought so! It's amazing how just five miles up or down a mountain can be such an obstacle to making friends. I never set eyes on your wonderful daughter till yesterday."

Dad touched his spectacles and then ran his hand through his thick, cow-licked, blond-white hair.

"That is true," he said with a slight smile. "About small distances being more significant out here."

For a moment we stood around awkwardly. Then Elodie, glancing at the bookshelf, exclaimed, "Walter Scott!"

"Do you like him?" Dad said. "We are not the most literary family, unfortunately, as you can see from the bookshelf. Some Emerson, the Apocrypha, a little Goethe, the Grimm brothers, and *Encyclopedia Britannica*—that's all I can stomach other than Scott. Amelia reads that set of encyclopedias as much as anything. I always plan to read more. But we love Scott, do we not, Amelia? Even though perhaps he is a little dry? My wife and I spent six months in Edinburgh before immigrating to the United States—passport issues, nothing interesting, but a difficult time. Perhaps Amelia will tell you sometime. It helped our English improve and I found I had an affinity for Sir Walter. He is well loved in the South, I hear. There are many of Scotch blood in this region."

"Oh indeed! I have Cherokee and Scottish in me—though I cherish my Cherokee heritage the most."

A question glittered in Dad's eyes but he withheld it for some reason. Sensing another pause in the conversation, I intervened:

"*The Antiquary* is our favorite Scott book. This is a first edition, can you believe it? What's your favorite?"

"Oh, fascinating; how rare! I love his poetry most of all, but that's his best novel, I'd say. I'm glad to know you have good taste." She chucked me under the chin. "Hmm…a good question. *Lady of the Lake* is closest to my heart."

After a slight gesture that changed her field of vision, she registered the dolls for the first time.

"What a collection you have!" she said, looking at me.

"Not Amelia's—mine," Dad said. "An old hobby. I buy them. Some new, some old. I make little repairs, that sort of thing."

"I see," she said. "Very interesting." She glanced over the dolls again. "Best be going? I'll take good care of her, I assure you. She tells me she's only been up to town about ten times so this'll be a treat!"

"I am sure," Dad said, with a slight, archaic bow. "Just have her home by dark."

We swung up the curves in the dirt road, following the mountain's dramatic switchbacks, the car shuddering and lurching. I gripped the side bar, fearing I'd be thrown out. Gaps in the rhododendron revealed seas of views, hunchback mountain upon hunchback mountain receding into cloud and blue haze. The wind gusting through the window carried the scent of the rhododendrons' pink and white blooms; the outside forest mingled with the car's smell. It was luxurious. Elodie's hair fluttered back, revealing a fascinating ear, swollen like a cauliflower. I'd never seen an ear like that before.

At the snap of a magician's fingers, we were in town. I couldn't believe it. All this time Elodie and I had been silent— but an intimate silence, a silence like a cord of mutual understanding and anticipation. Attic Window, it is said, is the highest town east of the Mississippi River. But that summer it could have been on the Italian coast. We passed the three-story inn, the pharmacy, the violet-painted house with the wraparound porch, the Masonic Lodge, the soda shop, and the hardware store.

"Home's just around the corner," she said. "I say we have tea—what do you think? We've got Orange Pekoe, my favorite, Earl Grey, and Green. Sugar and fresh milk, too."

"Sounds lovely," I said.

We passed the tiny gas pump of the filling station, which lay twenty yards in front of her house, and came to a stop by the whitewashed cruciform structure with a gable roof—not overly large, but at least three times the size of our house. Whenever I came to town, it reminded me that, in some ways, Dad and I still lived in a near-pioneer state. I followed Elodie through her immaculate kitchen and entered a side room. She led me to a glass case in a mahogany frame that must've been three yards long, nearly encompassing the room from window to window.

"Artifacts," she said. "My husband's and mine. It's how we came together, actually—this mutual interest."

The word husband stung me; heat rose to my face. I chastised myself, wonderingly, for being so silly. I hardly knew this woman. She was older and married and knew her place in the world. How different from me! A newly minted adult without social value or circulation; a girl with no prospects beyond the garden and the schoolhouse from which, I'd been made to understand, I might expect a position next fall if the current mistress moved to Kansas after all. It took me a few moments before I could follow the train of her monologue, which had already moved on from the first artifact—a quartz mortar for crushing spices.

Her finger smeared the glass directly above a bone pipe with a panther carved into the bowl and an extraordinarily long stem (the tobacco cloud that issued from its depths must've been enormous).

"...is a peace pipe, my great-great-grandfather's actually. God, it's beautiful. He brought it to New Echota for the treaty council but never smoked it there or any time after. He stayed with the Eastern Band of Cherokee, hiding out in the forest in that awful year, 1838—not far from here. Scott's roundup team made my great-great-grandad's brother execute a fellow Cherokee on the Trail."

"And what's that?" I said, not knowing how best to continue the conversation in that solemn vein and only knowing the outlines of this history. I didn't want to embarrass myself in front of her.

"An atlatl—for spear throwing."

"Your great-great-grandad's?"

"Not that. Atlatls are Archaic, much older than the Cherokee—this one could be 7,000 years old."

We walked farther along the glass case, pensively, as in a museum. We passed arrowheads, potsherds, tomahawks, and some clay objects I didn't recognize. She pointed at a collection of mica sheets. They had strange shapes I could almost identify but couldn't quite put my finger on.

"What are those?"

"Maybe the most interesting relics we've collected. I don't know. They have such a resonance for me, these mica figures. More for me than for Silas. But I suppose that's to be expected—his love for our collection is purely abstract. I feel like I've got a responsibility for them, strange as it may sound, given that I've only inherited one precious item and am as distant from that world and Qualla as Silas in many ways. I'm more Scottish than Cherokee—and more American than either (I noticed that questioning look your dad gave me). I may be just a white collector, but I feel a connection, a bridge between that past and this present, that my sisters don't feel—I've never understood why. They poke fun at me a lot. Anyway, a farmer found these mica figures oh, ten years ago at a place now called Mitchell's Mound. Then it was just a cornfield. Silas accepts artifacts, you see, at the grocery store in exchange for produce. Mitchell gave us these treasures for a pound of sugar and five jars of sourwood honey—can you believe it? Fallen on hard times. He found the mica figures in a grass mound, a tumulus they call it. Actually found *within* the bodies inside the mound. No exaggeration there—these were actually *inside* the dead, held in place by closed teeth like coins. And if you look carefully you'll see that all these mica figures are headless—humans, and animals, and maybe gods. That one right there is a man without a head—and that one's a bear, and that a panther probably, an elk, a wolf, a buffalo, and so on. The curves of their bodies cut as gracefully as my best china."

She had me in a trance. I was thinking back to the days— not so long ago, if the hunters' stories were true—when panthers, wolves, buffalo, and elk roamed the North Carolina mountains, which Elodie told me are called the Blue Smoke Mountains by her ancestors and kinspeople.

"Shall we have tea?" she asked, breaking the spell. "And then an adventure? Do you have time? For just a wee little adventure?" She brushed invisible hair from her face and made for the kitchen.

That day after tea, we went up Watauga Mountain, just outside of town, to a view called the Evening Door, where the hemlocks frame the western landscape. I'd never been there before, and Elodie was astonished at this, given that the trail branched off from the very same dirt road my house was on. There we ran into a pleasure party on horseback. The Japanese photographer George Takeshi, who lived in Asheville, was among them; Attic Window and its environs was, in the mid-twenties, becoming a destination for artists. Takeshi had a clean-shaven face and wore a red bandana; a monumental tripod lay across his lap and all sorts of camera equipment dangled from the saddle. Elodie made small talk with him since he'd photographed her and her sisters a few years back. I mentioned Dad's name and gave Mr. Takeshi our address, knowing that Dad would find great pleasure in speaking with another shutterbug, especially one so locally famous.

After they departed, Elodie and I watched the shadows of the mountains creep across the town and the gas lamps come spluttering to life. Soon the sky was brown and windy, like a winter sky in spite of the warmth. She got me home just before dark. When she pressed my hand goodbye I could hardly breathe.

Thus began our adventures in her Ford. She'd whisk me back to my house amid cicada music, right before the last vestiges of light left the sky and Venus caught us in its cold gaze. We spent less and less time in town. During that first month, I only met her husband once, even though the filling station was practically in their yard. He spoke softly and kindly to me, with a slight stutter. He was very short, had a mustache black as onyx and eyes of the same color; a beautiful man, no doubt. He wore a Panama hat and a brown suit. He reminded me, despite his beauty (and somewhat uncannily), of one of the cornhusk dolls Dad had at home.

My best memory of that time occurred at summer's end. Elodie and I had discussed going square dancing at Ogilvie's barn, but we decided a quieter evening outdoors was preferable. She let me take the helm and drive her car down the bumpy road that ran from Attic Window to Icecandle Mountain—a fairy tale mountain, aptly named—which is the crown jewel of this region. In winter, at sunset, its towers and buttresses, encased in an armor of ice, burn yellow like a candle. The car splashed through puddles and wheels spun; I swerved away from trees and boulders under Elodie's guidance. We couldn't stop laughing. We climbed higher and higher on the plateau until we came to Sheep Silver Cliffs, where we parked and made our way up the mountain on foot.

I pointed out wild ginger, mayapples, slime molds, turkey tail mushrooms, centipedes, and other botanical and zoological charms and curiosities. I pressed down on a devil's snuffbox mushroom and spores puffed out and made me sneeze. Elodie followed me over to a mass of blueberry bushes whose fruits were still green and unripe. She was entirely ignorant of the rich ecological web around us; I offered her the small knowledge I possessed and she received it gladly, though her retention for this sort of information—unlike historical names and details—wasn't the best. After marveling at the edibility of rock lettuce, she asked if I knew anything about this mountain's history.

"Only that legend about Sheep Silver Cliffs; how a hundred years ago a shepherd lost his sheep during a blizzard. Afterwards he found them, a hundred head or more, wedged in the narrow crack running from the top of the cliff to the bottom; all of his sheep had fallen into it."

"I've heard that one, too—exactly the same way. A man named Crunkleton? That's the one."

"What do you know about Icecandle? Dad visits here pretty often. It's hard to beat the view from the top."

"You said this is your third visit?"

"Fourth," I said.

"Well, geologists say that this mountain was once as high as Everest in the Himalaya. What's that? Twenty-five thousand feet or something like it? Of course it's been weathered down from an alpine peak to a five-thousand-foot nub. In Cherokee they call it Sanigilâ'gi or White Mountain—though some call it *Yonah*, since every October the mountain's shadow looks almost exactly like a bear. Legend has it that once this mountain was the foundation of a great bridge that spanned the region, arcing for sixty miles from here all the way to Unaka Mountain. Isn't that a wonderful thought?"

"It is," I said. "I've heard other things about it now that I think of it. Dad is friends with this old hunter named Pinkelsimer, who comes by and tells stories. He said that the last panther in North Carolina lived in a cave on the southern cliff. And that a witch lived in that cave after the panther died—that she was a kind of spirit of the mountain, and whenever Northern prospectors came to survey the quartz veins for gold, she'd change them into goats and crucify them on a tree. I'm serious! I can't believe you haven't heard that!"

Elodie was looking at me skeptically. But I resolved the matter by giving her a little push, which she returned.

Before we knew it, we'd covered the two miles to the summit, and walked along the edge, which migrated up and down according to the whims of erosion—the bell-shaped cliffs below us dropped and curved in dizzy combinations, vertical and then suddenly smooth and round as glass. Hawks circled and dove beside the cliffs, where they'd made their nests for the summer.

We sat down together on a shell of rock where moss had formed a cushion soft as sheep's wool. We linked arms and watched the mountain's shadow grow across the valley. We walked over to the carving allegedly made by one of Hernando de Soto's soldiers in the sixteenth century: "Un Luego Santa / A La Memoria." Elodie said there were arguments about its meaning: either "A normal walk for the record" or "In memory of a future saint." We debated whether it was real or fake. She opted for a forgery, and I, just to see her face flush and get my heart rate up and feel our minds grating pleasantly, played devil's advocate.

Sensing the sun disappearing, we walked farther along the mountaintop to a different overlook. Lightning bugs pulsed mustard yellow in the trees, and now and then a blue one cut across our path. The sun trembled on the distant mountains; its after-light spread red and gold wings across the blue-grey twilight. Elodie swiped invisible hair from her face, got up suddenly, and walked over to a dying, leafless oak tree with two forked branches. She leaned back against the trunk and stretched her arms out towards the heavens.

"Look, I'm the prospector. And you're the witch. You've crucified me."

"Don't say that," I said tenderly, going over to her, suddenly bold, pressing against her body, touching my mouth to her mouth, which fit so perfectly. I pulled away, feeling saliva stretch and break along our lips. I'd never kissed anyone before, but she seemed to guide me with invisible strings.

"I think you're the witch," I said.

"You're crying," she said, ignoring my retort and brushing a tear from my cheek.

"I didn't even know!" I said. "That's embarrassing."

"It isn't," she said, kissing me again and leaning her forehead against mine. "It isn't, my pet."

We stayed there long after sunset, watching the terrestrial constellation of a town come to life. It swirled so distantly, and in such a flat area of Georgia or South Carolina, I asked if it was Atlanta we saw. Elodie snuggled into my shoulder and bit my armpit lightly. "You crazy thing," she said. "Atlanta? My charms have confused you. That's just Walhalla, twenty miles away."

I can't record any more tonight. I've written myself back into stillness. Later I'll record the aftermath, the waves of calamity that followed that summer. But tonight I can rest again. I can enter the strange world of dreams, now no stranger than the reality of the woods beyond my garden. The fire and the patter of rain lulls me to drowsiness. I'll put down my pipe and swaddle myself in quilts.

Letter Folded in an Eastman Verichrome Kodak Film Box

Mr. Emil Hollwede
Hemlock Cove, North Carolina
March 10, 1938

My dear Emil,

I thank you again for the lovely surprise package. Herein I return the books you so highly recommended without, I might add, a scratch on them or a crinkled page. I'm honored you entrusted me with them. Sir Walter Scott is indeed commendable for his eloquence and broad, disinterested worldview, so I can understand why you so adore him, and the passages that appealed to me most revealed him to be a witty dialogist and vivid painter of wild scenery. I was least bored, believe it or not, by *The Monastery*, though I must confess I found it hastily written. The supernatural, ghastly elements I prefer, as you know, and was always itching to have more of them in *The Antiquary* and *Lammermoor*, though they certainly contained a few gratifying moments of this sort.

We have always been candid with one another, and I feel certain you'll forgive me if there is too much vinegar in my assessment. We have different tastes, and both of us are picky readers. I confess that I found the books overall dull, tedious, and showing innumerable signs of haste. Despite the vivacious dialogue, the characters are lifeless and I often had trouble untangling the Scottish dialect. I felt as though I were studying a Latin grammar book because the words are so long, stale, and legalistic. It is a fault of mine, and perhaps my sheer Americanness, that I cannot relate to the upper-class snobbery of a distant time and country. A ring of mold stained every page for me, even the best ones. I know this will hurt your feelings. But if I was not candid, and you sniffed me out, I know you'd never forgive my dishonesty. So there!

The family is well. I have had many pressing concerns so I hope you will excuse the long delay in returning your books. I was very glad to have the chance to scratch Mr. Scott permanently from my reading list! I look forward to your scathing remarks come October.

I hope y'all are in good health. Do give my regards to Amelia.

Ever yours,
Aura

[*scrawled on the back of this letter in Dad's handwriting*]

Mrs. Aura Mashburn
Macon, Georgia
March 21, 1938

My dear Aura,

Please do not come in October.

Best regards,
Emil Hollwede

Doppelgänger

In my dreams, a man's face passed back and forth across my bedroom window. His hair was white, his face droopy like melted wax; two rosy splotches were painted on his pale cheeks. It was a half-familiar face and didn't frighten me. He spoke in an accent I could barely understand. I could make out the words "after such a time" and "the private Madonna." Then Dad replaced the stranger; he took me under my armpits and, like a young man, tossed me into the air.

I woke refreshed. Yesterday, October 19, was an anomaly; so rarely am I sick, and so rarely, in the last forty years, have I mentally rehearsed the entire early history of myself and Elodie. Usually I just replay snatches and dwell on the worst moments. As I rolled out of bed, stirred by the bronze light invading the room and the uncomfortable silence caused by the birds' exodus—I've heard no birds in the trees for many days—the great emptiness left in Dad's wake pulsed through me again. I met the gaze of the cornhusk dolls I hadn't interred with him. I went and stood by his grave under the poplar tree and muttered the only poem we knew by heart, "Elf King," in broken and hesitant German. In this case, however, the poem's situation was reversed: the father was enticed into the gloomy place in the willows, into the elf king's land, and the child bereaved.

There'd been a light freeze last night; the corn stubble was covered in rime. I went out back and sawed and chopped wood for a while. I fastened a new axe handle and burned some brush. I tried to do other practical things—I fixed the rain gauge and chopped more wood until I worked up a sweat, but no matter how hard I labored, I couldn't extinguish thoughts of Elodie and Dad.

I made my way to his workshop to continue an examination of his photographs, wondering nervously which one would spark desire and propel me to new local mysteries. I hoped to God I didn't respond to a photograph of Attic Window. I wasn't ready for the crucible of visiting the town yet, not having been there in over fifty years. Who knows what changes and horrible truths await me there? I feel I must first comb the cove's secrets before braving the town. There must be some clue down here beyond the faces and voices in the landscape; if the orchardist could be seen and heard, a man who died long ago, why couldn't Dad be seen and heard likewise?

I dismissed the photographs of gourds and purple martins, views of Icecandle Mountain from Watauga, orchard blights, and the dim, grainy scenes of men with pine torches hunting bullfrogs on some midnight lake. The enigmas that pricked me, that twisted their surgical edges into me and wouldn't let go, turned out to be two photographs: the first of a wood-and-iron bridge across the Chattooga River woven with shadows; the second a view from that selfsame bridge, probably taken between its latticed railings, looking out at the ghostly river, trees closing around it and the brow of a waterfall just visible. A nervous glow rose from the pit of my stomach to my teeth. Both photographs had been cut by Dad into squares. I couldn't decide if they were taken recently or long ago. These were the ones, I thought; these were the coordinates to some untold place where the veil is thin, the partition between the known and the unknown eroded to a fault line. Perhaps Dad would be waiting for me there with a message from the beyond explaining why the world has broken and descended into a kind of delicate chaos; perhaps he had become the bridge, his soul transformed to wood and stretched across the river.

On my bike again, I passed the orchard and instead of taking a left towards the quarry, I turned right down the dirt road called Forestrum Road, which used to be maintained by the Forest Service. The sun, as I walked my bicycle up the steep incline, sat on the branches like a crystal ball. It was a sun I could stare at without hurting my eyes. When I studied it, it seemed to magnify, stretch, and invert everything (the landscape, me) within its spherical lens.

I coasted down the long snaking road, applying the brakes often, doing my best to maintain a slow pace as I wound toward the Chattooga River, which roared steadily and audibly a mile away.

As I thrilled in the windy freedom and pleasure of riding my bike, an image flashed across my mind that I couldn't dispatch: the Virgin Mary, surrounded by light, holding a cage. I let go of the handlebar and felt in my pocket, suddenly panicky, thinking perhaps I'd left the Virgin figurine at home. But no, she was there, the wood warm and pressing from my thigh like a rogue heart.

I dismounted at the wood-and-iron bridge. I checked its cracks and swirling grains for signs of a face and knocked on it, asking if anyone was home; I scratched on the rusty iron with my fingernail but received no response. That made me sad. I'd hoped another Hemlock Cove old-timer had transmuted into the bridge and could give me some encouragement or clues about the state of the world. My heart would have burst if that old-timer had been Dad and I could speak to him one last time; if he could give me hope that we'd meet again on some other plane of existence and all was not lost. I tried to stay positive, however, and stuck my head between the railings, gazing at the Chattooga River. Veils of water flowed across boulders. The river boiled and dove headlong into cavities, the rapids like white-maned horses with green bodies shattering against the rocks. Mica-rich sand glittered beneath the green rush, which sent gusts of cold air up to my face.

The last time I came here was with Elodie. The water had been high after a sudden thaw. She'd reeled off a list of facts, as was her wont, about the practice of logging on the Chattooga watershed. The details of that conversation I can't really remember. Something about the felling of old-growth trees, dynamiting splash dams, river men and skimmers riding and guiding logs down the thundering rapids by the thousands. Fragments like those. Long ago I would've given anything to be able to reconstruct that little lecture of hers, to recapture the feeling of that day and the dramatic curve of her waist. But not now. What I remember are the material things. How we scoured the white sand for branches to throw into the river. We lost sight of the black branches after we heaved them into a swift central chute, since their blackness merged with the dark green of the water; but the white, stripped branches were visible all the way down the tiers of rapids, twirling along the swerves and crashing against the rock walls, somersaulting over cauldrons, and riding the gushing weave of the waterfall down to the pool below the bridge.

I returned to the present. An object glinted at a bend in the river a hundred yards or so away. Something astonishingly white and crystalline—too white to be a boulder of granite or gneiss, unless it was a miraculous outlier.

I followed the trail that mimicked the contours of the river, twisting through forest and rising along miniature cliffs. I noted the burnt-looking bear corn and the proliferation of stalked puffballs, a curious, coral-red fungus that looks like it's covered in amphibian eggs and apple cinnamon jelly. The air became palpably colder; you'd think the north wind blew from the hollows of the trees. I crunched onto a maple leaf encased in ice. That was strange, I thought—the ice had grown a couple centimeters on the leaf's surface. An icicle hanging from a branch was suffused with the sun's dim light; the stumps of ancient chestnuts had accumulated snow, forming odd shapes like statues of disfigured children. As I bent down to enter an archway of rhododendron, a downdraft of snow blew upon me with a power like that of the adjacent river. It bowled me over and a cord plucked in my wrist. Then the snow passed and I was left in a garden of winter. But how could there not be a hint of snow in the autumn landscape except for here?

Nursing my wrist, I got up slowly, feeling my age. Loneliness swept over me. I wanted to sit back down but forced myself upwards and leaned against a snow-shagged branch. *Keep going*, I told myself. *At some point the unraveling of reality has to stop or you'll catch a flying thread. Your mind is sturdy enough to withstand these onslaughts of the unknown.*

I walked to a small crescent beach between cliffs where green icy slush beat against the golden sand. I noted that, a little way down the river, the autumn colors began again, flaring and lynx-eyed. The opposite bank's trees, however, were deep in snow and the landscape upstream was sparkling white. There must have been a freak snowstorm isolated to this one area.

As I turned back into the forest, snow exploded around me. For a moment I was blind, walking in a squall. Disoriented, shivering and my teeth chattering, I resolved to make my way out of this zone of winter.

When the snow settled, however, a wild crashing, followed by a thumping, echoed through the forest. I grabbed a branch to steady myself. I felt too sluggish to run. The noises got louder and closer, tearing through the forest's undergrowth. An enormous wolf with silvery brown fur broke through the rhododendron, heading straight for the river. I gasped. I'd never seen a wolf in these mountains before. Right behind it came a hare, whose eyes, I saw in a brief but intense glimpse, were aflame with a pure green light that did not contain the blemishes and obscurities of other eyes. Its paws left bloody prints behind it. Both animals slipped on the snow and slick rocks and splashed into the river current, the hare only a foot behind the wolf, both spluttering above the water then vanishing underneath.

Next, from the trail I'd passed down, from the south where autumn's last leaves still fluttered and clicked together, came a young woman. She wore a faded gingham dress that flared at her shins, revealing two muddy feet, red from cold in the patches of skin the mud didn't hide. She had dirty blonde hair. Her irises were large and brown like two acorn caps. Her cheekbones spread outward and tiny pimples gave texture to her skin. I let go of the branch and walked forward. My astonishment was too powerful to be afraid. This person was the exact semblance of me in my teens.

She stared at me blankly, not speaking.

I approached her. The river stopped crashing. It seemed to freeze mid-flight; then it started crashing again.

Pity, regret, and anger overcame my astonishment. I wouldn't ever want to be that girl again. Such a gullible, untethered little thing. So racked with insecurities, so far from the center of herself. I saw her as the girl who loved Elodie, who let Elodie ransack her soul.

Suddenly I lost control. A violence entered my being, a craving for abuse that blotted out all hope of reconciliation between me and my double. I closed the distance. My younger self hid her face in her hands. Such strength welled within me. It was a pleasure to pull her hands away from her face and shove her over. I mounted her, squeezed her lungs with my thighs and hit her with my knobby knuckles. Hair flew over her face, concealing her, but I brushed it aside. I wanted a full view. I pushed my finger into her eyeball, feeling its hot rotundity. She had no power to resist.

I would have performed an autopsy on her if she hadn't begun to disintegrate. I would have pulled her guts out like an impossibly long rope from a jester's box. My double, however, crumbled into twigs and leaves. Her hair turned to smoke and floated away. I fought on, snapping the twigs and ripping the leaves to shreds. Then someone restrained me. I turned, gnashing my teeth. I couldn't see straight. It was a person in old-fashioned clothing whose features were scratched out as with a pocketknife. I howled and wept, fighting this interferer, wanting nothing more than to get my hands on that crumbling girl again, yet my arms were straitjacketed. I weakened. My extremities went ice cold. The stranger's white beard fluttered like another downdraft of snow and the river crashed deafeningly. My mind darkened.

A Crumpled Paper under the Rocking Chair Cushion

Testimonial

I have been a wayward man. I have loved my daughter, even though she is quite grumpy and rude to my friends. She is a great gardener and forester and occasionally funny. Never once have I faulted her for her choices and mode of living when other fathers would have.

I loved photography. I was granted the gift of passion although none of worldly regard, which in hindsight was not a disadvantage. North Carolina is a beautiful state, even if the people are quaint, but I suppose I am also now quaint. I have loved many women but none as much as Rasma. My circle of friends was also a great love, though my temper often got out of control when I argued with them. I regret the fallings out I have had with many good people. Purple martins make me cheerful. When time permits I would be very glad to write to an entomology professor about the moths of the elm. I have lived here for many years but I have never seen such a swarm of moths as on July 2 by the mercury lights. Briefly I considered it to be snowing. It occurred for multiple nights in succession when Amelia was asleep and I did not wake her.

In case the remarks enclosed herein are improper, I apologize, minister. Do not be angry with me. Maybe there is a chance I will be saved after all, that the Madonna, who speaks to me and offers her solitary bosom, will intervene. I first heard the Madonna after the war but only listened, truly listened, these last three years when illness overtook me. On the morning of the summer solstice, above Devil's Courthouse, she stood atop a cloud, announcing herself as the Madonna of Carolina.

She gave me hope and ended my fear of death. For most of my life I did not fear death, but in my old age it paralyzes me.

Personally, Christ has always made me shiver like a heavy rain. The end is coming but I cannot tell my daughter. She will laugh. I have trained her to see knowledge as a ruin. Perhaps I was right back then and am wrong now. I do not know. I cannot unsee the visitation of the moths with the weeping faces on their wings that are migrating southward at the wrong time. That I could not collect any specimens upsets me. Frankly I cannot finish this testimonial as you directed.

Sir Walter's Tale

The old Scotsman raised his shaggy eyebrows when he heard me enter the living room. He put down the book he'd been reading and ran trembling fingers through his white, greasy hair and tugged his white beard. He opened his mouth and closed it a few times before finally saying with a Scots burr: "It is good to see you looking much better from that catch-cold, Miss Amelia." I had to focus all my attention to decipher his difficult accent. Since he discovered that I was an American, he'd modified his language, clipping away most of his "huts," "aghs," and "ye's."

I couldn't remember telling him my name, but we must have made some halfway coherent introductions during our trek back to my house from the Chattooga River.

"Yon library is a poor one, if I be honest, though there are a few choice volumes with which I have some acquaintance," he said with a smug grin on his face. "How the deuce do you get on here? Are you not bored to death? But this book by Miss Murfree is to my liking, as you guessed it would be, full of history and incident—the writing is not up to the standard of your Knickerbocker, whom I met once." His face became troubled. "I cannot recall the year anymore. Much has passed from my mind. I do remember our breakfast on that day—reindeer tongue, ham, corned beef, and eggs in the goodly dining hall of Abbotsford when I was Laird there."

I feared that this man would never stop talking nonsense, and leaned against the door casing. I could see by his expression that he was also irrationally afraid of me leaving him in the room alone again, amid the framed photographs on the wall that he kept eyeing with anxiety.

I mastered myself enough to say, "I can't thank you enough for helping me out of that mess."

"I couldn't do anything else," he said. His blue eyes shined, anticipating sympathy between us. "You were apoplectic and fighting a mound of leaves with a wan countenance and wild eyes."

"Well, just thank you. I'm surprised I didn't get frostbite. And you're sure I didn't hurt you?"

"Nothing worth mentioning."

"That's a relief," I said.

"And you still don't remember how it all happened? Why I found you ailing by the river?"

"No," I said carefully. "It's all blank."

"That's no small surprise," he said. "Now that the world's grown so uncertain."

He traced the swirling grains on the knob-end of his walking stick.

"I hope you do not mind, but I availed myself of a bath and washed my clothes as best I could. I feared I reeked of spoiled fish, and that would be more offensive to you than the liberties I took with the rites of hospitality. Under normal circumstances I'd never dare do such a thing."

I waved my hand and brushed the matter aside. "Of course you're welcome to anything around the place."

He smiled weakly and nodded appreciation.

"And these," he said, pointing to a black-and-white photograph given to Dad by George Takeshi, showing a sharp, twisted mountain peak somewhere in the Smoky Mountains, heaving balsam firs like dark lava into the air. "What machine made this? I've observed others in the little cottages hereabouts—which I entered, by the way, only because I found no one at home. I'm no thief, just a man overwalked. Far, far overwalked, with a lame leg to boot, and without my dogs or my daughters."

His ignorance of photography didn't surprise me. I had a feeling I knew who this man was, and that he wasn't from this time, that he'd passed on long ago; that I knew him like a friend or even a relative. I can't say exactly why I suspected this, but I was starting to believe that the world was coming to an end, or had already come to an incomplete end, and that the possible and impossible had ceased to mean different things, that they had joined hands in marriage or a fatal jump.

I explained photography to the Scotsman as best I could. His pale face grew paler and beads of sweat rose from his scalp and dripped down the white, forking straws of his thinning hair.

He asked me the year.

"1980."

He winced.

"Can you repeat that?"

I did. He limped across the room to the fireplace. He stood there, tapping his stick repeatedly against the andirons, muttering words I couldn't understand. He stared straight into the face of the clock on the mantelpiece.

"Can you fetch a pint of wine?" he said finally. "Or an ewer of water? And can we get a good fire going? I'll help bring in the wood, peat, or coals, of course, whatever you have out there. I'd happily be snug for the tale I have for you; if I don't tell it, at least in part, I'll go mad." And then he muttered to himself, "a tale more curious than ever I told in Martin Waldeck or Wandering Willie or in my *Monastery*. No faeries or *deils*, but by God enough devilry for ten lifetimes."

"I don't have any wine," I said, annoyed at being ordered around in my own house. "But you can get firewood out back."

He looked at me, confused. He swiped his free hand through the air, reminding me of someone petting an invisible dog. After a beat he nodded briskly. As he limped outside, I noted more fully his grey, slashed-up woolen pants, his dirty, stained waistcoat, his long brown coat descending below his rump, and his leather boots. I went to the kitchen and ran tap water into a mason jar for him to drink and to placate him, since he had, after all, helped me out of that bind by the river and probably saved my life. But a demon rising in my spirit, a repugnancy that I couldn't explain, made me want to send him away as soon as possible.

I heard him make a wrong turn around the house, but I didn't call out. Eventually he returned with an armful of poplar splits from the woodshed that he arranged in a careful pyramid on the grate. It took him a long time, his back bent and his movements labored. I wasn't in the mood to help.

"I've found on my long journey that this variety of wood gives a bitter smoke yet warms exceedingly well. I always keep flint in my pocket, mainly as a pastime, but God knows it has proved useful."

I handed him a matchbox. He looked at it curiously, turning it this way and that. He slid out the inner box and observed the rows of tiny matches with heads like inflamed pimples.

"Phosphorous matches? But much too small? I confess I don't know how to use them."

"Give them," I said. I snatched the box from him, striking the match once, twice, until a blue flame erupted. I touched it to the tinder pile, composed mainly of lint, already prepared beneath the grate.

The flames lengthened. He sidled up to the heat, propped his stick against the wall, and sat down on the hearth gingerly, hugging his creaky knees like a child, rocking back and forth, his face so waxy it seemed it might melt. He sat very close to the flames. I was afraid stray embers would eat through his clothes, and that whenever a log fell, he'd be showered with those little burning stars.

"I cannot restrain my tale any longer. It must bear forth. Miss Amelia, thank you, bless you in advance, for enduring the ramblings of a lonely, aged, ruined, embarrassed, lost man, without wife or children, kith or kin, without hope, without the frail fame of my former life as Sir Walter Scott, my crest utterly diminished...But hut! I must stay strong. For I was once a strong man. I could move the grand ebony cabinet at Abbotsford all by myself. I once punched a hole through a tollbooth door.

"In the last moment I recall clearly, it was 1832. I was sick at home, terribly sick. Oh God that home. I have seen much, but nothing like my own house, that I built from a cabin into a madcap castle, a flibbertigibbet of a house with turrets and battlements, in the distance the Tweed sparkling and the abbey ruins blue in the moonlight. I raved, they said, in those last weeks. In the moments when I returned to my own mind, I demanded a pen to write down horrible dreams of a society without order or harmony, the wand of anarchy quaking with power; dreams of vast forests usurping Scotland's wonderland of purple summer heather, great hardwood trees with octopus roots cracking the earth like an eggshell; but I couldn't hold a pen anymore, my hand shook, my mind wouldn't follow a straight line. What a difference! My way of life lost. The feast of fancy, as I once expressed it to myself, over forever!

"The dream of forests haunted me. I shook. I vomited. I cried out in pain. Was it death? No, not death. I listened to the light tap of rain on the latticed windows. Then my strength, quite suddenly, surged within me. I thought I'd received an electric shock. The hanging stair that communicated with my library glowed. I rose from my bed and followed that staircase, but it did not lead to my library and my thousands of annotated volumes. Nay, it led me down, deep into the earth.

"I never cared for a preacher or a priest, but when I found myself descending an unknown stair, I called out for one; I cried out for Christ, even though I never held religion or church in high esteem. I'd read the Bible, of course, through and through, there's no better prose in the language, especially in John. I imagined my dogs, all the ones who'd died, the dumb creatures I sometimes missed, God forgive me, more than my wife, accompanying me through the corridor, barking and leaping. Was I descending into hell? Had I become my own Steenie or Hogg's Dobson?

"My eyes, once keen as a hawk's, gave me no aid, and the effort to climb back up the stairs became too great. So down it was. Down and down, crumbling earth walls framing a narrow, sharply cut marble staircase spiraling into the ground, without the indentations of former footsteps. I leaned on my trusty staff, which I'd somehow managed to seize on the way out of my bedroom. By the smallest increments, each step downwards released a sand grain of weight from my mind and body, until I felt light as a wraith…I felt eerie, as my people say, but swift, tireless, driven.

"I required no water, no food. At some point the staircase grew level and the steps vanished. The path undulated as though I passed through a tunnel under a range of mountains. Sometimes the earth shook. At first I heard the drip-drip of water droplets from stalactites; later the rushing and crashing of a subterranean waterfall; and long after that a delicate lapping, then a heavy booming that sounded like it came from the ocean. At times I worried that water would crash through the cavern walls and drown me. I journeyed farther, getting used to the idea that I was crossing a continent deep underground or perhaps had discovered a tunnel beneath the Atlantic, a kind of subterranean Northwest passage. My thoughts, usually prolific, hummed pacifically like bees drunk with smoke. I floated on, only the lameness from my childhood bout with polio reminding me of my physical body. I never once rested but marched tirelessly onwards. Time lengthened infinitely or contracted to a grain of dust. The journey was all.

"I recall only one moment when this peacefulness was interrupted. A woman with skin like mirrors appeared in my path, lighting up the tunnel with her own inner light. My reflection broke into a thousand fragments across her body. My former intelligence swarmed back. This, I thought, is the god that summoned me here. I fell to my knees and raised my hands in supplication, but the celestial apparition froze as though caught in an act of robbery and gave me an embarrassed look. She turned her back. "I am not undressing!" I cried. "Do not go! Guide me, help me, save me from this doom!" She wavered, flickered, and vanished. If I had not been under the powerful spell of the journey, I would not have recovered from that blow, as I was in mortal agony; but as it was, I soon regained my equilibrium and pressed on, largely forgetting this specter. Now and then, however, when I stumbled, I felt the firm pressure of a cold hand steadying me.

"I must've wandered beneath that ocean for more than a century. But finally, the long ramble through gloom after gloom ended. The staircase emerged again from the smooth, undulating path, and rose in high, sharp steps for many thousands of feet and came to a dead end. For the first time in a life age my legs ached. A ladder half-embedded in the earthen wall gave me purchase enough to climb upwards. With each rung I ascended, the weight of my body returned and the millwheel of my mind spun faster—until the wraith I'd become over the decades pulsed with piping hot blood. With anxieties and gnawing memories. With a fear of falling. With a resolution not to lose my staff at all costs, despite the difficulty of climbing a hundred-foot ladder with it in tow—it had been my companion so long. I climbed to a ceiling where light leaked under a rock. I pushed this rock and it shifted. I pushed again with all my might (I was once accounted one of the strongest men in Roxburgh), and lo and behold, the rock fell backwards, uncovering a splash of blindingly blue sky.

"Dirt pattered down, and I crawled out, gripping the hole's edge for dear life, spitting pebbles and leaf grit. I tossed my staff from me and it landed a few feet away. I pushed myself up with all my might, lifting a shaky leg to the hole's edge to generate extra force. I made it and collapsed beside the piece of granite that had stoppered the hole. It took considerable time to get my bearings and for the world to stop spinning, but when it did I noticed trees, thick trees with healthy crackling bark larger than I'd ever seen in my life, receding one after another into a distance darkened by mountains not so different from those in the Highlands, but perhaps loftier.

"I used my staff to stand up. There was something familiar about this place, yet familiar like dreams or previous lives are familiar, nearly real, with textures of memory, but elusive. This wasn't Scotland. This was far from the Border, which was no great surprise given the enormity of my journey. No heather was in sight; no abbey ruins, no castles, no cottages even. The sun, dimmer than I remembered, wobbled like a shaky stone between the branches. I made my way out of the glen and eventually found a sort of sheep path, though, barring two notable exceptions that I'll recount in just a moment, I've never seen sheep, or a single animal for that matter, since setting foot on this continent which I soon discovered to be North America."

Sir Walter paused his narrative, wiped sweat from his forehead, and looked around the now-bright room. The flames shook strongly on the logs; glowing embers flew out and died on his lap. I realized he was searching for the glass of water. I retrieved it for him, feeling kinder and a little more patient. He gulped it fiercely and thanked me. He scratched a brown age spot on his pale cheek. For a split second he reminded me of Dad near the end when he was sick and shaken.

I sat down beside him on the hearth's warm brick.

"Go on," I said, "though I think I can guess the rest. Or a lot of it."

"Very well and very likely. You are ever a good listener and friend. So where was I? Ay, ay…it wasn't long ere I called out for joy upon seeing a house. A curious red one, with a steeply sloping roof, shaped like an upside-down V or a pediment—I believe I saw a sod roof house very like it once in a book of Dutch illustrations. I rapped on the door; I peered through the windows and glimpsed things I'd never seen before—strange objects and pieces of furniture. I was at a loss—yes, even me, who once was known as the Wizard of the North—was at a loss to describe them. I felt the emptiness, the dizzy anguish of my predicament, flood every branch of my nerves. It was all wrong. Who'd ever heard of a fate like mine? No Bible or legend ever told of such happenings.

"Like a thief I forced open the door. I called a greeting again and again. No one answered. I searched the premises— no one to be found. I went back in the house and examined the strange machines and glass boxes with handles and buttons. One of them was shaped like an old silver snuff box I owned but lost somewhere in Italy. Once or twice grey lighting forked across a machine's glass. I sat down on a comfortless couch, one of the few things familiar to me, and fell into a feverish sleep. After a dream of my Charlotte, the bride of my youth (but not as she was in youth—rather as she was on her deathbed, her face yellow and drawn), placing guineas on both my eyes, I awoke. My eyelids weighed down on my sockets like iron shells and I had to peel them open with my fingers. The first item my sight fixed upon was a chart or rather a calendar. At the top in black ink, I read "1979: Ten Year Anniversary of Lunar Landing, USA." Below this heading was the most naturalistic painting I'd ever seen: in the background a curved, milky, rocky landscape; in the foreground a human, or an orangutan for all I know, dressed in a white uniform with a white cushion on its back, descended a ladder, one leg hanging a foot above the rocky white surface. What the ladder was attached to I couldn't tell; it resembled hundreds of clumped mirrors. Underneath the picture was printed "Astronaut Edwin E. Aldrin, Jr. descends from the lunar module to the moon." I read this again and looked at the image. I read it thrice. I noticed the American flag in the right-hand corner but with far more stars than before.

"I puzzled over this for a time, but the conclusion appeared rather obvious. The evidence of my surroundings, and that supplied by my intuition, told me that I'd traveled beneath the earth nearly 150 years to the shores of the United States of America. Having read many of Knickerbocker's volumes, I wondered if I'd alighted somewhere in New York, or if I had in fact ventured farther west. I had two choices. Follow the inclination to blaspheme God and give myself up to madness or exert my rational faculties, which had always served me in abundance—to piece together this puzzle and show the courage native to my heart. I began to suspect that this might be my own personal hell, or that Hume wasn't mistaken after all, that the future is entirely unknowable and science based on false principles of consequence. I wondered, too, about Paley's argument for design—what if a man, this man, came across a pocket watch in the heath too late, and it had rusted, and the little wheels and gears God made were broken and beyond repair?

"I kept despair in abeyance. I sought out other people in the neighborhood. I followed a road. The sun had a strange muted hue. The leaves of the twisted bushy trees were strange, too, lifting in the wind like the green wings of grasshoppers. The great trees, the pines and oaks and species I didn't know, cast shadows like grey doors on the ground. I thought my heart would burst through my chest by the time I summited a mountain to get the lie of the land. What I observed astonished me. The mountains resembled pebbles on a riverbed, round cliffy mountain after round cliffy mountain to the horizon's end. And forest. What forest! Never-ending. Unlike anything I'd ever seen. It took my breath away and was too beautiful to be hell.

"I descended another glen and found more habitations with astonishing arrangements of windows and roofs, architectural styles utterly new to me. I encountered shining machines whose uses I couldn't fathom stranded in the amazingly uniform, rock-hard roads. Long black strings looped and drooped from wooden poles, stretching one after another like crucifixes along the road. The houses were all well-made minus a few small, sagging, dilapidated ones, again constructed with materials new to me. The sound of water was the same. The wind was the same except for the ways the trees strained and filtered it.

"What gave me the most pain was the lack of people. I thrive on people, you see. On the ways they clash, how high and low intermingle, how society is layered yet whole like a wedding cake. The lack of people made me despair for my sanity if my luck didn't alter very soon. Rain came, the crisp leaves fell, I fed on berries I foraged in the woods. On occasion I heard the distant chimes of bells, and the clopping of a horse's hooves, but never met a soul; I impute this to my overheated imagination and deep longing for my own country. With effort I climbed a lonely apple tree in a forest so golden you'd think a giant's treasure chest had spilled out upon it. I tried to read pentagonal and diamond-shaped signs in the roads. I began to feel as though I was walking in circles, stumbling upon the same houses with the same machines I couldn't operate. Every time I walked in one direction for too long, I felt as if a powerful magnet repelled me. I tried to make my way back to the tunnel I'd exited, to the rock I'd removed, but couldn't find it again.

"Until one evening I came upon a sequestered place, a garden that wasn't neglected; the stars shined on a rather simple though lovely wooden house with a high stone chimney. Curtains draped the windows though there were gaps here and there. Through a window, I swore I saw a figure prostrate on a bed. I flicked the frosty glass pane and felt shock when something moved, a slight rolling over or tossing. Do not startle the person at this ungodly hour, I told myself. You don't want to make an enemy, creeping up to a window like a murderer in the night. Bide your time. Wait till the morrow.

"Yes, it was your home, Miss Amelia. The story has at last found you. I'd borrowed a blanket from a nearby cottage and slept on a mattress of springy, dry moss a stone's throw from the little beck from which you must draw the sweetest water. As the sun rose in some unseen quarter, I could barely discern your home coming into outline between grey branches. I waited anxiously, then grew sleepy despite myself. I dozed. I awoke when a door slammed. I glimpsed you walking toward the road, then mounting a wheeled machine. I hastened but couldn't catch up. I called but you did not hear me. I limped after you as best I could. Soon, however, I lost you. When the road turned to dust, I followed the marks left by your machine, eventually finding it abandoned by a path leading into a wilderness resounding with a river's thunder.

"Despite my trusty staff, I tripped many times on the steep grade, became tangled in thickets, in what you have called rhododendron if I remember rightly—a plant I've seen in Scotland, but never so woody, dense, and massive. The banks grew wetter, the going more treacherous. The air grew colder, too, as happens when one nears a rushing mountain river.

"My lame leg, which usually doesn't ache awful much, hurt more than usual in this deep cold, and I limped more than I had since I was a lad. The green water, so different from the dark glossy water of the Tweed, swerved and broke along shores of sand and boulders the size of shepherds' cottages.

"Quite suddenly there was a tumult in the wood. It was like a fox hunt with the pursuers charging close behind. I expected to see horses break through the brush any moment, but instead galloped a giant, beautiful wolf and behind it—I swear I don't lie—a hare, throwing saliva like birdseed, hot on the wolf's tracks. Perhaps I'm in the end of times, I thought, where the order of nature is backwards, since, contrary to Isaiah, the beasts do not live in friendship and the lion does not lie down with the lamb. Here, the lamb pursues the lion; the prey pursues the predator. And it dawned on me that perhaps here was a sign. Maybe, instead of a curse, a miracle had been sent, by God or who knows what, to lead me to you. As the pair disappeared into the trees, I followed their trail. Not an over-difficult task, since they kicked up all the leaves in their fury. The leaves fluttered up to the trees and rocked downward as if the twigs had dropped them a second time.

"I entered a land of winter. As I moved farther into this landscape, following the hare and wolf tracks in the snow instead of the kicked-up leaves, the temperature got colder and colder until my bad leg felt like a block of ice with the nerves intact. The pools I passed were frozen to flint. At some point I heard the river crashing clearly again and walked towards it.

"There you were, Miss Amelia, thrashing, fighting a mound of leaves and not comprehending my entreaties. I restrained you momentarily, and you fought me off like a powerful wildcat, but as soon as you'd overcome me bodily, you broke away and fainted. I tried to revive you—all for naught. A cold sweat drenched your limbs and I feared for your life.

"Your face, aged like mine, reminded me of an angel's in the way it glowed in that winter landscape. I tried to lift a mask of wrinkled glass from your face, but there was no place for my fingers to catch. What an illusion! I could swear that a child's face showed forth beneath a glass mask, and that the signs of age were tricks. I do not mean to offend. It's hard, I know, to admit we are old when we feel young at heart.

"At last I succeeded in reviving you. You rose to your full height, a stately straight-backed woman, well over five feet. Forgive my impertinence—I sometimes find myself describing people as though they are characters in books. A bad habit. Well, then, we stumbled away from that winter place. You tried to climb atop your two-wheeled machine, but I begged you to desist, to stay with me, that you could retrieve it later. You yielded to my entreaties, complaining of a headache and confusion, and guided me along the roads on foot to your house. It took many hours and you showed great fortitude. You refused to take my staff. Sometimes you raved and called me father, but for the most part you were lucid. When we arrived, you bid me welcome, and implored me to wait here in the living room and to eat whatever I liked; that you could take care of yourself and please not to disturb you for some time. You needed solitude as well as rest. And as you can see, I granted you that.

"That is my tale, however unlikely it may sound. But I feel confident that you don't think it impossible. That you believe. So now, perhaps you can help me. I'm desperate for answers. Bless you again, Miss Amelia. Finding another human at long last is sweeter than honey from the rock."

I lied to Sir Walter and said I suddenly felt tired. I told him to sleep on the couch (I didn't want him to profane Dad's room). I returned to my bedroom and got under the covers and lit my pipe. I hadn't thought to offer Sir Walter any tobacco, but I wasn't going back out there.

I need to understand this new bead on my fate's rosary. Very few people, so I've heard, have had a single encounter with the occult in their entire lives. In the past week, I've had more than I can count. It is as though a light shines on my mind, and silhouetted in the near distance are fragments of ideas connected by a shadowy logic. If I had devoted myself to one tradition, to the cult of the Virgin, say, or to the mysteries of Faerie, would I have been whisked away by some rapture? Is that what's become of everyone? Have they met their gods? Have I been abandoned with sweaty, rambling Sir Walter? A man out of time, whose novels once meant so much to me but whose physical presence I do not desire. I'd assume he was an imposter if my intuition didn't declare otherwise. Is this apocalypse for me and the Scotsman alone? Or is that just solipsism? I'd give anything to meet another woman, to see Mossie Reynard, perhaps, the only one of Dad's friends I ever felt nervous around, with her crystal skin and red mustache. I'm awash in old dead men. Sir Walter isn't the companion I want.

I've reread that scrap of paper Dad left under the rocking chair cushion a dozen times, and it points its finger resolutely at the Virgin or rather the Madonna of Carolina, who has no precedent in any gospel I know—whether in accusation or benediction, I can't say. Will she stand behind the final gate? Or will Dad? I experimentally pray to this Madonna of Carolina, asking for forgiveness, if she was the mirror-coated apparition Sir Walter saw, if she is manipulating me, but receive no answers in response, no indication she's listening: only a hissing mental static.

When I take the figurine of the Virgin from my pocket, the cross on which she was suspended is gone. Her other breast is missing and she is flat-chested as a boy. Her black shock of horsehair is also gone. All that remains is a writhing, bald figure with arms held upwards as in victory.

Attic Window

In the twilight of the next morning, I got up to make breakfast. On a shelf above the sink sat the two cornhusk dolls in front of a little cabin made of sticks and moss. The woman doll wore a plaid button-down dress with a high collar, miniature copper eyeglasses, and a bonnet. The man doll had on a Panama hat and corduroy suit, with a black mustache made of horsehair and eyes of the same material rolled into tiny balls. With all the clanking of dishes, cutlery, and swift whisking of cornmeal and buttermilk, I hadn't heard Sir Walter come up behind me.

"Good morning," he said. "Interesting figures there!"

I dropped the mixing bowl into the sink. He put his hand on my shoulder to calm me down, but I batted it away, stammering, "Thank you, it's fine. You just scared me. And those dolls, you mean? They were my father's."

"Forgive me." He bowed his head. I noticed that his temples carried indentations like fingerprints in beeswax. I had a mental image of him awake all night, pressing his fingers deeper and deeper into his head.

"Don't worry," I said. "I've forgotten about it already."

"They remind me of a figure I once saw at a quaint thatched cottage at Gallow Hill, between Leith and Edinburgh. It was made of clay mixed with paste. Brass pins had been thrust into the figure's bosom to accomplish a deed of black magic. A peasant's wife, Bessie Gowdie by name, attempted to murder her stepsister through such vicarious means...though I assume such petty deceptions no longer dupe the scientific mind, in your country as well as my own."

"The dolls aren't for witchcraft," I said, a little amused and offended. "They gave a sense of community to the household and made things less lonely. These are called cornhusk dolls."

Sir Walter looked at the dolls intently for a moment, then closed his eyes and nodded. Wrinkles layered his forehead. I could tell painful thoughts were firing across his brain.

"Sit down," I said gently, gesturing to the table. "We'll eat. Just some cornbread and autumn olive jam on crackers. I don't have any eggs right now."

"Thank ye, thank ye," he said. "I'm hungrier than I ever was after a long ride in the morning."

I poured oil in the cast-iron skillet, put it in the oven, and started boiling water for tea. I asked him, "Whatever happened to what's-her-name with the dolls like ours…Bettie? Was that it?"

Sir Walter tapped his walking stick on the linoleum. "Ah, Bessie Gowdie. *Convicta et combusta*. Convicted and burnt."

My stomach shifted like a bag of sand. "Was that normal back then?"

"That was one of the swifter punishments. The drawing and quartering and pond dragging were lengthier methods of torture. But that's not a matter for the first breakfast shared by new acquaintances."

There was a pause and I asked, "Did you sleep well?"

"Not exceedingly well, though the couch was comfortable. Fatigue, a rheumatic headache, and all the—what's the term—photo-graphs in the room kept my mind in a whirl through no fault of your hospitality. It vexed me not to hear birds of the night and the morning. An uncanny place this is."

"Do you mind me asking," he continued after another pause, "who Emil Hollwede is? I've noted his signature on the frontispiece of some of your books. Your late husband?"

"No, my father. He recently passed."

"My sincere condolences," Sir Walter said. "And that's why you live alone, I presume. I, too, know the ravages of loss. My heart breaks when I think of the bride of my youth, the poor mamma of my daughters—as well as a dear friend or two and my dogs, as foolish as that sounds. I cannot believe you don't have a dog or an old tomcat on the premises. The gentle beasts make life jollier!"

I remained silent. I didn't confirm his presumption about my solitary life. I couldn't bear to speak of the little stray cat I'd taken in and loved with all my heart, and who died alone when I was out gardening all day. Sir Walter withdrew into his own inner world while I opened the oven door, poured the cornbread batter into the skillet, shut the oven, and set aside the whistling kettle.

At breakfast—after requesting, very humbly, more bread and honey—he began to ask me specific questions about this area of North Carolina and world history since his time, and I answered him as best as I could. He asked me if I could supply him with any old ballads from this region of America. I could only remember a few snatches I'd heard at school, which I recited to him. The song that begins "Come in, come in, my old true love" and the one about how when "a woman's single she can live at her ease." Dad and I weren't musical types and, because of Dad's German heritage and my seclusion, my relationship to Appalachian folklife was different than most. And despite Sir Walter's express wish for me to continue, I could tell that my ballads were only half listened to, and my accounts of civil and world wars and bombs and moon landings had shaken him to exhaustion. He was growing paler by the minute. I asked if he felt strong enough to take a stroll, perhaps a long one, up to Attic Window, the town on the mountaintop not four miles away.

"A town! I've wandered this region for many days and nights and never once caught sight of a town. Do you think anyone is there? I'm starved for conversation, for knowledge, and it's unfair to place all the burden on you. Let's set off at once. I am strong, dauntless, and if you are up to it, let's hasten there."

While I felt nervous about being responsible for this man, given all that was on my plate (so much was happening that I had no interest in asking him about his life, his famous friends, and his novel writing), I decided that I could not face the town alone, that I needed a companion. He would be useful, helping to steel me to enter the place I hadn't visited since the Elodie days. Being responsible for him would give me courage. I also desperately wanted to know if Attic Window contained the answers I'd perhaps been avoiding by remaining in Hemlock Cove.

The mailbox, stuffed with old letters from Carolina Power, pizza ads, and other junk mail, was the only pitstop we made before venturing up the road. We followed the snaking curves of asphalt, both of us stopping to lean against trees on the roadside. After a couple hundred yards I proposed we check out the Hemlock Cove Poplar, the second largest poplar in the world, that was fifty yards down a dirt side road the CCC had built. He assented and made some comment about primeval and inaccessible American forests as we touched the pocked, ancient, five-hundred-year-old bark (it took four people with linked arms to encircle the trunk) and gazed up at the thick, half-hollow limbs, twisted like chicken joints, overshadowing the understory of pines.

We continued up the road until we came to the house of some summer-only residents of Hemlock Cove. I led Sir Walter up the driveway to their little green house, in front of which a dirty beige Oldsmobile was parked. I opened the unlocked car door. Sir Walter inquired about the machine's function, and I explained it to him as I searched for the key, which naturally wasn't in the car. I peeked in the house's front windows but saw nothing worth noting on the kitchen table or countertop.

Nobody stirred within. I decided that, even if I found the keys, it would be too much stress to drive. I wasn't even sure I could anymore—I'd probably drive straight off the mountainside. So I tugged Sir Walter's sleeve. He was inside the car, tinkering with the steering wheel; he accidentally honked the horn and banged his head on the car's ceiling.

We trudged on up the mountain road. When the grade was steepest, Sir Walter thrust himself up rather awkwardly with his walking stick. The going was slow, and I often thought about how I'd driven up this road so many times with Elodie during that lovely summer long ago, young and nervous and flushed with the enormous potential of life. Eventually, with a view of the champagne-and-blood-colored valley below, with its granite fists and branching creeks, the road humped, then leveled out, and descended. A whitewashed store, which hadn't been in that spot when I was a girl, cheered our prospects up ahead.

"By God, tartans!" Sir Walter exclaimed, seeing a display of plaid in the shop's window. There was no sign out front, only a yellow note taped to the door's inside pane that read: "The Wee Shoppe closed."

"A friend once told me how the first European settlers around here were Scottish," I said as Sir Walter examined the kilts in the window, clearly with some misgiving, since his look was growing skeptical. "Not Scotch-Irish, but settlers from Jacobite times." He turned to me with a glitter in his eye. "I think that's right," I continued. "And I read somewhere, probably in an encyclopedia, that the Scottish and the Appalachian Mountains, long ago, maybe in Pangea, were part of the same mountain chain."

"Counterfeit tartans even here," Sir Walter muttered. "Spread over the whole kingdom and the world. But tell me more, Miss Amelia, about the Jacobite immigration to this place. And the geological theory you just mentioned. That interests me greatly. In fact, I left Lyell's book on my desk at Abbotsford."

"That's all I really know," I said.

He humphed and followed me as I rejoined Main Street. We had to climb one more hill before arriving in the town proper. The top of this hill was the true summit of Attic Window Peak, and it made the town of Attic Window the highest east of the Mississippi River. A stone marker informed us that we stood at 5,124 feet. On the way down this little summit hill, we saw two dozen whitewashed and red brick buildings, a church steeple, and gravel parking lots with abandoned cars. Nobody walked about the streets. It was completely empty. I breathed a sigh, whether of relief or disappointment, I can't say.

The morning sunlight became even more silvery than usual, and leaked away with each step we took towards town. Had the trees grown especially high? I looked around at the hemlocks. Was a church steeple blocking the light? By the time we reached 4th Street, where the buildings conglomerated, hardly any light remained. You'd think we'd journeyed around a curve of the earth. The upper arc of the sun was in view, resembling the moon more than the sun; it seemed to shine with borrowed light and was speckled with craters. I realized with a slight shock that I hadn't seen the moon in quite some time. I usually spend the evenings in my house writing this account, but still, wouldn't I have noticed it at some point shining in the window?

A strange wind blew down 4th Street from the north, the direction of Icecandle Mountain. It smelled yeasty. Wild. Reminiscent of tart berries, leaves, and the guts of insects. It blew strongly and nearly bowled Sir Walter over. I steadied him. His eyes rolled back and forth as he adjusted to the sudden change of light and the powerful current of gamy wind coming from the north.

"Excuse me," he said weakly. "This is the abode of Eolus himself, or my wits have gone a bell-wavering."

I told him to sit down on a bench. I made my way back up the hill we'd just descended. There, I had a full view of the sun. I could see its dim electric orb a quarter of the way up the horizon. I could swear cracks threaded across it like a netting. When I walked down the hill, the world plummeted back into purple semi-darkness as though the sky were wrapped in plum skin.

Saliva dripped down the corners of Sir Walter's mouth and accumulated in the curled mustachios of his beard. His blue eyes flickered over me. Halfheartedly, I put a hand on his shoulder, and he responded to that. He seemed to click back into reality and see me again. "Miss Amelia," he said with an affection that made me uneasy. He looked at me like a sweet, abused, needy dog. I wanted to run. I needed this man, at least for the time being, until I got my bearings and regained my confidence and sense of self-reliance, which, after the debacle with my doppelgänger, had faltered somewhat. This was a person to share a broken world with. Why, after all I'd been through, with so much pain and solitude, with nature's laws rewritten and many signs pointing to the end of times, would I want more than anything to be rid of him? But that's what I wanted. The way he acted reminded me of an ailing father or budding lover (and I could never be a man's lover).

"Let's go," I said, trying my best to be civil. "Let's see if there's any food to be had at the grocery store. It's just up ahead. We both need something to eat. Though we won't need to go shopping or stockpile any food—I've got enough cans and jars in my cellar to last many years."

"I think I need a second breakfast," he said. "I'm going mad…I certainly am. I felt a fracture back there, as if I'd fallen from the top of a lighthouse and struck my head on a rock. I don't know what caused it, if it was that ghastly wind or apoplexy. My power of speaking was taken away. If that happens again, I fear I'll lose my grip on reality and be brain-sick for good."

"Don't think that way," I said, understanding that fear wholeheartedly. "You'll be fine. Just come with me and I'll get you a snack and a drink. That'll make you feel a lot better."

I could see him mulling over words like grocery store and snack, but he seemed to get the gist and was too exhausted to ask more questions. We continued on at a halting pace. The road was narrower than it had been fifty years ago. The great oak tree and fountain in the middle of Main Street were gone. Above intersections, black poles hung that I realized must be traffic lights. A few cars occupied parking spaces. The grocery store was still in the old place, except that it had been expanded and now boasted glass windows across the front.

I opened the door. Unsurprisingly, the place was deserted. I got Sir Walter to sit down at a table in the front. I searched up and down the broad shadowy aisles, full of all kinds of boxes and food I'd never heard of before. The floors were spick and span as if newly mopped. Nothing seemed out of order. I glimpsed Sir Walter staring from his table at what must be the cash register, which had a starkly different appearance from the ones in the past resembling typewriters. I opened a cooler that was warm inside. Bottled Cokes and canned Cokes crowded the bottom. After laboring at a bottle top, I popped the tab of a can, which my cousin Tempie had once shown me how to open. The acidic bite on my palate was sharper than I remembered, but soon my throat was thickly coated as with molasses. It made me feel sick but in a good way. I popped a tab for Sir

Walter and gave it to him to try. He took one sip, swished the liquid around his mouth, and then gulped volubly. He had a strong question mark in his expression. I couldn't help but feel amused by it. After swallowing he coughed. You'd think he'd taken a shot of whisky. He nodded his head and took another draught. I left him sipping the Coke to find some food.

All the vegetables had turned brown. Bubbles of liquified rot had formed around the celery and broccoli crowns. The other perishable foods, and especially the meat, were covered in molds and ran with dark liquids. I gave up looking for something healthy to eat and picked up a box of Ritz crackers, which Sir Walter consumed with less relish than the Coke he'd already emptied. Crumbs dribbled down his white beard. I motioned for him to brush them away, but he didn't take the hint. He looked so dirty, so unlike Dad, who shaved every day. Sir Walter's beard grew unevenly, greasily.

"A strange repast!" was all he said.

We snacked for another ten minutes. Cracker crumbs turned his beard pale brown. When we finally left the store and headed out into town, the light was like that of a solar eclipse on an overcast day.

We passed the boarded-up shop whose basement used to be the Attic Window Darkroom and entered town center. Memories flashed across my mind. I thought of the time the circus came and set up in this very spot. I was fifteen. There were canvas tents, mamma and baby elephants, and a wagon painted with a zebra and a maniacally laughing clown. The living double of the painted clown sat atop this wagon, banging a drum with one hand and holding an umbrella with the other. A woman wearing a Robin Hood cap blew a trumpet. Each child, including me, held a balloon. The children at school had worked me up, making me anxious to go to this event. Dad took me gladly. I remember feeling—not unlikely by the other children, but not necessarily wanted. I felt on the outskirts and intensely sad for the elephants with men sitting on their heads.

A sign for a coffee shop caught my eye. Not seeing a bench for Sir Walter to sit down on, I instructed him to stand for just a moment while I went inside to see if I could find a newspaper. It was very dark in there, much darker than the grocery store since there were fewer windows. Nevertheless, I managed to find a stack of the local newspaper, the *Window Gazer*, dated October 3, beside the coffee lids, sugar packets, and honey. I eagerly perused the front page and subsequent pages. No information about a catastrophe; no great war; no prophecies of a Second Coming. The front-page story told of a ten-year-old boy and his father who'd drowned after sliding together down the cascade on Kalakeleski River, having got their legs wedged beneath an underwater boulder. Other stories recounted board meetings, the woes of the high school basketball team, and a controlled burn near the Chattooga River, the Forest Service warning of smoke hazards near Olto the week of October 7. There were no indications of what had happened to the world, no news beyond the day of Dad's death. That didn't surprise me, really, but made me sick at heart, as if someone or something was observing everything I did and thought. I left the shop and found Sir Walter leaning against his walking stick, gazing curiously at me. I recommended that we take another break. There was an antique shop a few doors down. He brightened up a touch.

"An antiquarian's shop! Very interesting. Say no more!"

I opened the jingling door of Wolfgang's Antiques and was greeted by a collection of porcelain dolls with cherubic faces and clown dolls with red and blue stars painted over their eyes. The interior of the store was as dark as the coffee shop, but my search behind the counter yielded two flashlights. I switched them on and gave one to Sir Walter, who said

"Marvelous!" I left him slashing his beam like a sword, studying with deep interest the watercolors, antique mirrors, dog figurines, leather-bound books, urns, and other random objects. He kept sighing with pleasure and catching his breath in wonder. I turned my attention to a shelf of new and used books. I thumbed through a novel from the forties called *Moon Mountain*, passed over a set of Thomas Hardy novels, and picked up a large art book called *Cult of the Virgin*. There was something familiar about it; I had a vague memory of seeing a book with a similar cream-colored spine on Dad's nightstand, perhaps a year ago, but couldn't say for sure.

The spine cracked pleasantly. It clearly hadn't been opened many times. The glossy pages were beautiful. The first image that arrested my gaze was a Renaissance painting of the Virgin, with downcast eyes and flowing chestnut hair. She stood atop a moon surrounded by storm clouds. Stars encircled her head. Her lavender dress gathered and creased along the moon's upper curve, hiding her feet from view. Her fingertips touched delicately in prayer. The image on the next page showed a Virgin in a maroon cloak, spreading her arms wide like a bird about to take flight. Tiny worshippers no bigger than her hands kneeled before her and gazed reverently. The third painting, however, pricked me with a sense of foreboding, as though it were a glimpse of the future. It showed a monk in a white cowl with his hood thrown back. He spread his palms wide to the Virgin standing on an altarpiece. An ugly, curly-haired Christ child was ensconced in one of her arms. With her free hand she squeezed her exposed breast; the pink nipple was puckered between her fingers, a jet of milk shooting from the nipple into the open mouth of the monk.

I flipped through more pages and a postcard fell out. The painting on it was much less skillful than those in the book, and I wasn't entirely sure what I was seeing at first: a Virgin standing on a green hill sprinkled with azaleas, blue watercolor mountains lapping the sky? There was more, however, and my hands began to shake. This Virgin balanced on only one leg. No—she was, in fact, split in half, right down the middle. She held a lily plant, with its white flower drooping against her shawled head like a telephone receiver. She gazed upward with one eye, one nostril, one hand, and just one foot of her own. The crude painting was titled *The Madonna of Carolina*.

The postcard's back contained handwriting: Dad's elegant cursive. There could be no mistake. It read: "Almost there. The harvest sun. Look up. The gauntlet nearly run."

I imagined that the figurine of the Virgin, still inside my pocket, produced a steady heartbeat. I almost expected her to climb out and dance on the floor. Anything could happen now. I rose quickly to leave and didn't even pocket the postcard—I felt overburdened with artifacts as it was.

The flashlight's beam groped across the walls and revealed Sir Walter examining a letter opener with a bone handle. I told him that I was leaving. He tried to detain me and point out a few items that had come from Scotland, but I burst out the door into the open air. The wind coming down 4th Street could still be heard, whistling like a gale through a narrow, invisible gorge.

"Did something happen?" Sir Walter asked, blustering, trying to catch up but failing as he limped down the road.

"I need some air," I called back. Hardly were those words out of my mouth when I came to a storefront that blazed with light, as though my presence had summoned it. The light blinked and fizzled. It came from a smooth glass square encased in wood. Dials and switches spread across its bottom. It occurred to me that this machine must be a television. Dad's friends often spoke about them. The square light even reminded me a little of the luminous cloud that had risen from Dad's corpse.

On the screen, fuzzy, indecipherable images flared and disappeared in quick succession. How this TV operated, I don't know; none of the light switches had worked in the grocery store or in the antique shop. Sir Walter, who had now caught up, flashed in and out of the semi-darkness. The TV shot out a beam as from a lighthouse's mirror, catching me in its radiance. Sir Walter stood mesmerized, leaning on his walking stick. His tongue crept out of his mouth like a snail.

The television's light was accompanied by no sound. A red button glowed like an evil eye. Inside the glass, I thought I saw a clown, a man wearing a costume in the style of Pierrot, sliding his hands down the dazzling bare shoulders of a woman wearing the rosary. A blank snow blew across the glass. Then my image, my very own worn old woman's face and long, white, frizzy hair, came alive, somehow, inside the machine. My face grew more distinct until the television screen zoomed in on my loose, wrinkled dewlaps. Instinctively I touched them with my hands; as a girl I swore I'd never have a grandmother's turkey waddles. But there they were. That's okay, I thought. There's no one left to impress. There never really was anyone to impress in the first place.

Sir Walter glared at me with knitted brows. The camera now focused on my face, then cut to a shot of a figure arrayed in white, floating inside the giant sharp-toothed maw of a whale or perhaps the mouth of some crystal cavern. She—for it was a woman—wavered in a white, brilliant, smokeless fire. Her face was young, then old; a stranger's face, then my own.

"She's in the box and outside the box," Sir Walter muttered.

I was too mystified to comment.

"Guardian of the paths," he continued, blue veins radiating across his pale face. "Work thee ill." He rocked back and forth as in a trance and recited in a quiet baritone:

Neither substance quite, nor shadow,
Haunting lonely moor and meadow,
Ours is the sleep that knows no morrow.
The molten gold returns to clay,
The polished diamond melts away
All is altered, all is flown…

I hated hearing people recite poetry (whenever Dad's friend Max started that sort of thing, I'd unapologetically leave the room). I pried myself away from the television and entered the storefront, shining my flashlight around the electronics, plastic boxes, silver antennae, and newfangled radios. I cried a hopeless greeting and beamed the light here and there. As I exited the building, Sir Walter swung his walking stick and toppled over, releasing the stick so that it knocked against the display window. He sprawled on the sidewalk, comically spread-eagle.

Had he swung his walking stick at me? It all happened so fast. I couldn't tell. I couldn't believe it.

"I am bewitched!" he said, moaning. "Of such things I was once incredulous, but now…here…"

I helped him up, even though part of me wanted to leave him there. He did not thank me for getting him back to his feet. Tears swam in his eyes. I bent over, retrieved his walking stick, and handed it to him since he was wobbling.

"This afterlife," he said. "It has been such a cursed business. Perhaps a business nearly finished, or I flatter myself. I can't last much longer. Egad! What I would have given, what fame relinquished, to die peacefully in my bed at home, and not stranded, or trapped by some spell—I don't know—in another time and country not for men of my ilk. Has my devotion to the Almighty been deficient? Has my poor churchgoing led me to this purgatory? Art thou the Vivien to my Merlin, the very incarnation of the White Lady I abandoned? Are my Sins incarnate?"

I didn't understand most of what he referenced, though I recognized the White Lady from his novel *The Monastery*—was she a demon or the Virgin Mary? (It has been so long since I've read that book.) I walked away from him, past the place where Elodie's house used to be and that they'd turned into a public garden; I shot a quick glance at the miniature torii gates and stone lanterns that stood in the place of that once beloved spot and fought back a surge of bittersweet nostalgia. I was still enamored with the spot after so many years. It made me angry at myself.

I marched down Main Street toward the cliff where the town ends abruptly, where the road winds down the gorge alongside the thunderous Kalakeleski Falls. I popped my head into every shop and house and called hello, sweeping the rooms with my flashlight. Near the town's end, I noticed a strange haze where Main Street turned into Cliff Road. Sir Walter lagged far behind. I heard him coughing and stabbing his walking stick into the asphalt.

Quite suddenly, directly before me, a barrier—milky, gelatinous, and semi-transparent—rose in a wall. It hadn't, as far as I was aware, been visible from the center of town. But here it shimmered with a smoky electricity that pulsed in waves, cutting off access to Cliff Road, the only way out of Attic Window from this direction. I turned around and saw Sir Walter standing stock still.

I could sense neither cold nor heat coming from the wall. I touched it experimentally. My fingernail burst into flames. I jerked it back, screaming, blowing out the flames and sucking on the burned skin. I squeezed my finger to make sure I still had feeling in it. The nerves weren't damaged, but the skin was seared with second-degree burns—a pain I wasn't totally unfamiliar with from many cooking blunders. Sir Walter must've heard my scream, but he hadn't made a move. He formed a shadow on the road above me. I could feel him squinting his bad eyes.

I could not see the hemlock trees or the old post office behind the barrier. They should've been there. Another kind of landscape lay behind this wall: intensely red, shrubby, and hilly.

And then something rustled behind the barrier. Four people, I thought at first. But then realized it couldn't be, that the shadows striding along the other side of the wall moved in unison. It was a woman on horseback. Silver bells hung from her horse's mane. She was naked. Her hips curved dramatically; her arms were chubby; her stomach emaciated; her breasts small, tight like knots of wood. Her hair dark as night and her mouth so wide that its corners could be connected with straight lines to the tails of her eyebrows. It was a relatively young face but ruddy, wrinkled with care, as though pencils had drawn lines at random but not necessarily followed the normal wrinkle patterns of aging humans. The horse drew her along the other side of the semi-transparent wall. I yelled greetings and questions at her. How could I get across?

I waved, not daring to get too close to the barrier and burn myself again. She lifted a hand but never reined in her horse. The silver bells hanging from its mane jingled distantly. I followed her along the wall, flailing, pleading, asking her wild questions, begging for her to impart her knowledge if she had any. Did people live on the other side? Was she alone? Would the world always be this way? Was the Virgin Mary or Madonna of Carolina responsible for the current state of things?

The woman, however, seemed to forget my presence as she veered off into the shrubby hills. Her back muscles tensed and relaxed with each step the horse took. I hollered at the top of my lungs. I searched frantically for a keyhole or a breach in the wall but found none.

I came to myself sometime later, weeping on my knees involuntarily. My finger ached and throbbed.

The hair on the back of my neck prickled. I had an intuition that Sir Walter stood above me and that he'd just arrived at this spot. I looked up anxiously. I was right. There he was, with sweat on his brow, his face flour-white, looking strangely determined. His thoughts, I could tell, were a world away from mine.

"I must take my leave now, Miss Amelia," he said in a hard, crusty, affected tone. "I can read you now like a newspaper." He thumped his walking stick on the asphalt. "There are things beyond the reckoning of mankind. Dark miracles, it appears, persist even into this future time. I know now you are one of them—an agent of the shadow world. But I do not ken what to make of that yet."

The Bronze Road

The dogwood trees had bloomed white, and daffodils, bluets, and spring beauties sprinkled the grassy roadsides with the first colors of the new year. Wisteria draped the trees in purple colonies and drugged the air with erotic perfume; the smell reminded me of root beer. Yellow pollen made wave patterns across the windshield even though Elodie had wiped it off that morning with a wet cloth. We drove down Route 23 towards South Carolina. The Ford jostled and jogged and spit forward and decelerated abruptly. She was an expert at not stalling the car and guided the hand throttle with ease as we wove down the mountain roads. The engine purred and clicked with a steady rhythm, and even where a freshet from the previous night's storm had submerged a dip in the road, the car splashed through it gracefully. The curved granite face of Nikwasi Mountain was like a giant turtle shell greyed with age and lichen.

Elodie wanted to show me something—a sacred place that meant the world to her. Her dark hair, which she'd let grow long, danced across her face. I gazed at her beautiful round nostrils shaped like marble molds, her lips that were always chapped. We'd been lovers now for ten months. Everyone thought us the best of friends. Dad was the only outlier, the only one who seemed uncertain how to process our relationship. His jade eyes had observed me bustle about the house getting ready for Elodie's arrival. He'd looked up from a book he couldn't focus on.

"No need to destroy the house," he'd said. "Certainly Miss McWaters can wait if you are not ready. Yes, you look fine as always my dear."

Elodie hung a right onto a dirt road gullied out from rainstorms and hillocked with duff. We bounced up and down, the tires spun and miraculously escaped swathes of mud. A turkey bobbed across the road into the rhododendron thickets. The Chattooga River boomed in the distance, beyond a mountain or two, and I could tell we were somewhere near the South Carolina border.

"Aren't I doing good not asking where we're going?" I said. "It's hard. I keep checking myself."

"You know how I like to surprise you, my pet."

Hearing that phrase gave me a swirling sensation. As we went along, I couldn't tell if I was carsick or lovesick. We didn't speak for the last twenty minutes of the ride, just observed our surroundings, reclined in that atmosphere of ease and desire, and eagerly awaited the first signs of the hidden river.

She pulled over seemingly at random. Why here? I noticed nothing special.

"A secret place wouldn't have a trail marker," Elodie said, observing my uncertainty. "For once I get to guide you through the woods, and I don't have to hear your well-meaning directives…watch out for this, here's my arm, that rock is slippery, that root is tricky—oh no, now I'm the leader."

The bank plummeted steeply, and we had to hang on to rhododendron and mountain laurel to reach the bottom without injury. We passed through briar patches, thorns etching blood beads into our skin. I was surprised Elodie knew where to take me in this fragment of wilderness—she was a town girl minus her interest in the occasional archaeological dig. The trees ended in a circle of grassland, a meadow stowed in the forest's pocket. A ruinous clapboard barn, with stray boards dangling from alley doors, projected above the grass. Old potato cellars, springhouses, corncribs, and smokehouses, ruinous also, dotted the meadow along a thirty-yard arc. It didn't look like much to me, just one of an uncountable number of deserted nineteenth century farmsteads in western North Carolina. Springs undergirded with rainbow-colored stones gurgled from the earth, and a creek rambled along the perimeter of the property and, beyond the trees at the meadow's limit, emptied into the Chattooga River.

"Here we are," she said. "A place I've come to since I was little. My grandfather took me here. It's a testament to my love for you that I'm showing you such hallowed ground. It's not just an old homestead. This was Chattoogie Town, a Cherokee town. Some say the Creeks destroyed it in the 1750s. Afterwards, a solitary Cherokee man lived here until a minister from Charleston bought the land from him—or more likely swindled or bullied him out of the property."

She left me and hunted about the grass. She bent down, rooted in the ground, and held a piece of muddy pottery to the light.

"Little People, I want to take this," she said.

I couldn't help laughing. "Are you serious? I never knew you to be superstitious."

She said nothing. I came up behind her, hasping my lips to her neck.

"Not here," she said crossly.

"If it was a Cherokee town like you say, I'm sure thousands of people wooed and made love here."

"Not if. When. And now it's a site of desecration. Though can't you feel wonder, like a slow-turning tornado, moving about this place and plucking at your heartstrings? But maybe it's not that way for you."

It wasn't like Elodie to wax so poetic. Her excitement moved me. I closed my eyes. I could feel something ancient stirring me, but my thoughts remained cloudy, indistinct, detached. A wing of darkness swept over my heart. For a moment

I couldn't breathe. I felt more distant from Elodie than ever before, as if she lived on another continent and all the boats had been burned, and not even bravery and the willingness to undertake a long and difficult journey that would likely claim my life could lead me to her again. Melodramatic, I know, but when I opened my eyes a tear glided along the curve of my nose into my mouth. Elodie didn't notice.

"My grandfather," she resumed, "my dad's dad, brought me here when I was a girl. He died when I was four, so I don't remember much, except that he took me by the hand and crouched down, guiding me to the earth, and placed my hand on the soil, telling me to listen for a heartbeat. He told me to repeat the word *Kituwah* and gave me a name that I cherish but can't ever tell another soul—not even you. In our culture women are sages and warriors, and he blessed me with a panther's subtlety and strength. He led me down there"—she pointed—"about two hundred yards, to the secret waterfall. Few know about it. I'll take you in a moment. Just know this is something I'd do for no one else. I haven't even brought Silas down here, and I'm carrying his child."

I snapped a look at her belly, which wasn't swollen. I'd noticed nothing the week before, when I'd spent an hour with my hand splayed across her stomach, my fingers gently squeezing the birthmark an inch above her bellybutton; it was like a miniature bird crushed by a thumb. I'd stroked and kissed her. I'd lapped the pooling sweat in the thimble of her navel. But I'd never guessed there was an inhabitant beneath. In my naivety, I'd assumed she and Silas never had intercourse. That idea stung me. My mouth became dry. My inner world shuddered on its axis.

"It doesn't change anything," Elodie said.

She took my hand and pulled me towards her. She drew me across the grassy meadow towards the trees. The sound of the river was like loud static on the radio. I had trouble generating a coherent thought until I found myself at a ledge. A deep, bowl-like cavity opened a hundred feet below us. From the ledge, a woolen waterfall left the river's plane, spiraled through the air in its headlong descent, and crashed into a village of boulders. A rainbow bent across the waterfall's spray, which, even at this height, misted our faces. I had to continually wipe droplets from my eyes.

"There's a cave behind the waterfall. Can you see it?"

I latched onto her words as best I could. "I think so. Maybe."

"Come look at it from this angle."

She took me by the shoulders and guided me in front of her. She leaned her chin on my collarbone and pointed.

"Ah, right. I see it."

"My grandfather told me this is a very sacred place. That the footprints of Little People, and many curious and unknown objects, have been found in the cave behind the waterfall and that maybe it's a gateway to another world. My grandfather's grandfather, a man named Atagâhï, once told him a story, or a lie, as my people call it, about how he'd heard whispers coming from the river, and that he'd followed a road within the river, a road made of bronze. He'd passed under the mist's rainbow, past the waterfall's veil, and into the cave. There he discovered a hundred loaves of hot bread. When he picked them up, they shrank in his hand to acorn-sized cakes, the most delicious he'd ever tasted. Atagâhï ate them all except one. Then a door of darkness opened, beckoning him to pass through it to the world of the Nunnehi, the immortals, and live in their never-ending country beneath the mountain. But Atagâhï was wise, even as a boy, and refused. He left the final bread loaf as an offering and passed back through the waterfall by way of the bronze road beneath the Chattooga, returning to his village. Though a boy of seven, he came home with a long white beard. It was the bane of his life, shearing those hairs from his face every morning."

As she told this tale, it seemed that wind blew from inside the cave, originating in some other world, puffing the waterfall outwards. I could smell clouds, venison roasting over a fire.

"Can we look?" I asked nervously. "I think we can make it behind the waterfall—I see a way right there. It doesn't look too dangerous."

"Absolutely not," Elodie said. "I've given you enough. I told you: not even Silas knows of this place. I've never told him that story. And I don't even know if I'd be allowed to enter the cave. If the immortals are still there, would they whisper to a woman who has lived her life in an American town, who doesn't know the Cherokee language, whose heritage is nearly lost? They might embrace me; they might spurn me. And I couldn't handle that. But if I had to place a bet, I'd wager the Nunnehi are gone forever—or maybe there are a few left in Qualla or Oklahoma, where some say the spirits followed my people on the Trail, weeping along with them as they were driven out of the mountains, turning back to look only once, for a second time would break their hearts."

I didn't really desire to enter the cave. It scared me. I had asked to show Elodie how much I wanted to be with her and to understand.

By the time we reentered the meadow where the ancient village of Chattoogie once stood, the sun had set. The moon was a lavender thumbprint with a silver fingernail. We slammed the car doors, not looking at each other. Then she closed the distance between us like a bird of prey. Between kisses, she thanked me for coming with her. She sucked my earlobe, and I lifted her blouse, searching for the birthmark near her navel. We made love awkwardly and unthinkingly, sprawled across the front seat. We supped with passion and desperation until the lights of another car beamed nearby. We quickly put our clothes in order and swung out of the gravel pull-off, driving back up the mountain, racing ahead of those headlights swooping through the trees.

I stuck my head out the window. My hair was pulled back by the wind and fluttered wildly. I shouted at the car behind us, feeling reckless. I made honking goose noises. I bleated like a sheep.

Fingers clasped my dress and I fell back into the car.

"Quit being a fool," Elodie said. "What if someone sees?"

"You haven't cared about that before," I said, offended by the way she'd yanked me inside and the tone of her voice, and not knowing whether she meant someone seeing my odd behavior or seeing us together.

"You're not my mother, you know."

"Thank God," she said. "I couldn't deal with that all day."

"Yes, Mrs. Fenton."

I knew calling her by her husband's last name was crossing a line. It was an unspoken rule that she always went by Miss McWaters and nothing else. Because of the darkness I couldn't read her expression. Had she been making a mean joke? How angry was she? And was she genuinely relieved I wasn't around her all the time because I was too immature, too much of a nuisance? Her attitude towards me had changed suddenly, irrationally. I wished I could read her mind.

We only spoke again when she pulled up to my house: just curt goodbyes and then her headlights fading down the road.

Dad didn't wait up for me that night. He'd left a simple dinner of tomato stew on the stove. I went to bed, however, without eating. I was not usually one to skip meals, but I couldn't shake the sensation of impending doom. Even though Elodie could be grumpy and severe, she had a tender side, too.

I already regretted speaking crossly to her. I wanted to cuddle and make up immediately. Never before had someone eaten to my very core, hollowed out a place for themselves and made a home there. But her pregnancy, I just knew, had to cut some of the strings that tied us. In the back of my mind I feared that Chattoogie Town was some kind of parting gift.

Days passed and Elodie didn't write or drop by for an impromptu visit. I wrote a letter to her, expressing my love as I always did, but received no reply. We didn't have a telephone back then, so, having no other means of getting in touch, I decided to walk the four miles up the mountain to Attic Window. The road hadn't yet been blasted and paved, so it was more like walking a wide trail. It was a Saturday, and the town was bustling more than usual. Cars drove down Main Street almost bumper to bumper, and the doors of the shops tinkled repeatedly with the entrance and exit of customers. I ignored the stores and the heavy fragrance of sandwiches since I had no money with me, but I did stop at the circular fountain where the trout swam. I splashed water on my face, and drank a little of the water, despite the stares and guffaws of a gang of riotous boys who called me a "bumpkin" and said "that water warn't for drinking."

I walked on the opposite side of the street from Elodie's house. When I neared it, I crept along, scouting out the situation, fearing she'd catch me spying. I'd never visited her uninvited before; usually she picked me up at my house. I glimpsed movement on her front porch and darted behind a streetlamp. An old woman wearing a mink hat halted for a split second and looked at me inquiringly; I waved her away, annoyed and embarrassed, and she moved along. I peeked out from the lamppost. Smoke drifted up into the porch's rafters. Elodie's dark hair rocked in and out of view; another woman, with long blond hair braided intricately, brandished a cigarette. Elodie doubled over, laughing, slapping her knees. I couldn't determine who the other woman was since I could only see the back of her head.

I felt like I was falling with no one to catch me, so jealous I wanted to scream. Without waiting any longer, I marched back home, my brain buzzing with dark, circular electricity.

Elodie appeared in our driveway the day after this episode. I didn't tell her what I'd seen because I couldn't give away how much power she wielded over me. I pretended that everything was normal; she acted preoccupied. She dropped the name Exie when I asked her what she'd been doing the last few days. That rang a bell. I'd heard of this Exie, a young doctor who'd recently established an open-air sanatorium in Attic Window. I immediately suspected Elodie was having an affair with her, but tried to douse the thought. Throughout the afternoon, with less gusto than usual, Elodie swore that I owned her heart despite her pregnancy. She just needed Silas to have a family. He had lovers himself. By the way she addressed this subject I guessed they were men.

In the weeks after Chattoogie Town, Elodie laughed less, seemed less free of spirit and more distant when she picked me up in her Ford. It was as if, by showing me a secret, she had given too much and had to retreat. I felt I couldn't reach her as easily, though there were glimmers of the old correspondence: a few giddy frolics in the woods where no one could see us. I, too, began to act out of character in a much starker way. I became obsessed, paranoid that the love of my life would soon leave me. I collected stray black hairs I found on her sofa, in her car, and on my dress, and stole little items from her house that she wouldn't miss: cubes of sugar, odds and ends from her makeup supplies—lipstick, a pocket mirror, and a cotton handkerchief decorated with tiny North Carolina state flags—a cardinal's feather from one of her hats, stray cigarette butts on the porch (which she only smoked when Exie was over), a fingernail clipping or two, a ripped white blouse she'd thrown in the rubbish, a chip from a porcelain teacup, and a pair of stained undergarments.

Most days, after I'd labored with wheelbarrow and vine, and while Dad was preoccupied reading the newspaper, chopping wood, tinkering with a camera or out taking pictures, I'd go into the deepest recesses of Amelia's World, all the way to the seam where forest meets granite dome, not far from the derelict cemetery from a hundred years back, with its unmarked headstones and footstones; the sun cast crooked shadows here that didn't conform to the land's shape. About a hundred yards along this seam between forest and rock, I built a shrine to Elodie in a natural niche. The miniature cave must have once been a fox's home judging by the tufts of reddish hair and stone-hard excrement inside.

I'm still ashamed of it, but one day I went into Dad's room and burrowed into the very back of his closet, locating two cornhusk dolls buried beneath the mass. On one of them I painted carmine lipstick along the vegetable mouth. After I carefully removed the mustache and glued-on Panama hat from the other doll, I crafted a smile on it with Elodie's fingernail clipping and made a new little hat with the teacup chip and cardinal feather. I hid the mustache and original hat in my tackle box.

I constructed dolls of my own as well. I tied strings around Elodie's cotton handkerchief and used the cigarette butts to form eyes. I set up the pocket mirror in the mountain's niche so that two of the dolls shared the glass. I also constructed several figures with sticks and clay. Into them I kneaded strands of Elodie's black hair. I didn't do any witchcraft. I didn't believe in that sort of thing. I simply wanted a private place where I could go and be with fragments of her life, which was slowly draining from mine like a let vein. I feared her leaving me to an extent entirely disproportionate to the real harm such a deprivation would cause. The way I was acting, you'd think a massive meteor had been discovered in the night sky approaching earth. I slept with Elodie's undergarments wrapped around my hands like scrolls traced with sacred writing.

As I sank into my obsessive dread, the summer leaves unfurled and the world was clothed in green. I harvested the early plants, the radishes, carrots, cabbages, garlic, and winter onions. During mornings and evenings, I spent matins and vespers at the shrine at the back of our property, praying to whatever gods would listen, or to the strength within me, to maintain the fire of our love and let it flourish through whatever darkness. Dad was not one to spy on me, but he certainly noticed my absences and marked the direction of my walks. While Elodie wrote love notes to me and left them in the mailbox, she invited me over less and only picked me up for a brief adventure once a week. In the penultimate letter I received from her, she called me "my doll" instead of "my pet." That's when I knew for certain her devotion to me was waning.

On another occasion I walked to Attic Window. I watched Elodie leave her house, a noticeable hump in her belly, looking radiant and confident. She got in her Ford and drove off. She left in the direction of Judaculla and didn't return. I waited until midnight before finally heading home. Dad waited up for me, and asked where I'd been, but I just told him I was stargazing atop Devil's Lozenge. He examined me skeptically. He said he would say no more except that he loved me no matter what, and he didn't want my heart to break. I rushed into my bedroom, furious at him for mentioning anything about Elodie. I stayed up all night in a feverish, obsessive state.

The next day he asked me if I had seen his two cornhusk dolls, the man with the mustache and Panama hat and the woman with the copper glasses and bonnet. I said I didn't know where they were—he knew I wasn't interested in his dolls. He looked nervous. He turned over the entire house looking for that pair. He had trusted me without hesitation. He kept saying "I got them from Lully and she doesn't make them anymore." My chest burned with guilt and regret but I couldn't bear to tell him the truth, especially after that initial lie. If I returned the dolls secretly to his closet, he'd know it was me. And he'd certainly notice the slight alterations I'd made to their appearances, and the weathering effects of the errant gusts of rain that occasionally entered the shrine.

On a note scribbled hastily on a postcard showing Grandfather Mountain's twin peaks, Elodie said to expect her the coming Sunday, that she couldn't visit before and had been away on some business; that she would fill me in on everything when she saw me and had some exciting but painful news to relate and not to worry. Everything would be fine. She signed it "Your friend always." Dad had left the postcard for me on the kitchen table and I hadn't noticed it until evening. He was likely on the way home from a photographic jaunt; I vaguely remembered him saying something about a fallen tree dragging a car up onto its root ball.

The fireplace blazed. An axe edge of anger scored my mind and I threw the postcard into the flames. But just as quickly I retrieved it without burning myself and blew out the dancing flames. A black, ashy crescent had eaten away the sky in the postcard's corner.

Sunday arrived. I waited all day, pacing up and down, my mind blurry with anxiety about what Elodie would say. I told myself not to worry. Her having a child wouldn't change anything. Maybe the painful news was about the baby or Silas. She loved me more than him. I'd devote my life to her. No one else could give what I was willing to give. She knew that. I went around weeding the garden absentmindedly, missing large tufts and bruising my knuckle with the trowel. I stayed outside until the moon rose, then ate dinner with Dad, who afterwards brought me a warm towel and told me to lie down. He checked on me throughout the night. Eventually I fell into a restless sleep.

I woke at first light to the hoots of mourning doves. I pulled aside the curtains. My heart leapt into my throat, and I almost sank to the ground; what I'd seen, however, wasn't Elodie's sleek black Ford but Dad's smaller, more commonplace one, splattered with mud and parked in a different spot than usual. I rushed out barefoot and took the little path through the woods, one like elk might have made a century ago. I leapt over Quartz Dwarf Creek, just barely splashing my nightgown. I threaded my way through the labyrinth of trees, past the cemetery, across the boulder fields, to the rim of the granite dome, an offshoot of Devil's Lozenge eclipsing the old-growth trees in height by only a hundred feet. I struck the matches I'd left under the lip of the niche and lit a candle. I bowed my head and whispered, "Let her come, please make her come."

The cornhusk dolls lay on their backs staring at the shrine's ceiling. The handkerchief doll with the cigarette butt eyes had crumpled against the wall, its head bent to the ground. The one with the hat made of the teacup chip and cardinal feather had fallen to its side. The only doll to have retained its position was a clay figure with a fragment of bark pressed to its balloon-shaped paunch, representing Elodie's pregnant stomach and her ugly-beautiful birthmark.

I must have fallen asleep. Rain misted my face. I shivered. A branch cracked; a rock slid down a pile.

"…told me you were back here somewhere, that you come all the time," she said. I didn't catch the first part of her sentence. For a moment I had trouble getting my bearings. "You've taught me to be quite the wilder-woman—the path you made back here was pretty easy to follow. Aren't you proud?" She gave a little curtsey that, combined with her half smile and stilted way of talking, seemed fake. She wore the same white-collared shirt as when I'd first met her, or one like it, tailored to give more room to her stomach that curved from her midsection like a gibbous moon. Her black hair had been cut into a bob. She looked like a regular city flapper from the magazines.

The cobwebs cleared from my mind.

"No," I said.

I got up and pushed her back, away from the shrine. Two muddy handprints stained the shirt above her breasts.

"What's wrong with you?" she said. Her blue-golden eyes widened. She examined her shirt. "You ought to be ashamed. What's back there? What don't you want me to see?"

I stood my ground, blocking the path. She bent this way and that trying to peer past me, but I kept shuffling to get in front of her in that narrow passageway between the boulders.

"It doesn't matter," I said. "This is my sacred place. Just like Chattoogie Town is yours. I don't want to share it with you." My voice trembled. Tears started from my eyes. It made me angry that I was so weak. "You didn't come when you said you would. You haven't been writing."

"You don't know the meaning of a sacred place. You don't have a past."

I stood there in silence for a moment, glaring at her.

She lowered her eyes. "Forgive me." Then, reconsidering her apology, she said, "What's back there? Let me see."

"Why don't you just go fuck Exie," I said. "You whore." I knew I was crossing a line but couldn't stop myself. I hadn't spoken words like that in my own head even in my darkest hours. "I hate your history lectures and your phony upper-class act and your goddamn selfishness. I don't know why I love someone so selfish. You're the most selfish person I've ever met."

I burst into tears. I must've sounded like a donkey heehawing. I'd thrown open the cabinet of my heart and was showing her how she occupied every corner of it. Her power over me was limitless. It made me sick that she knew how desperate I was for her love.

She held out a hand, hesitantly, to cup my face and calm me down, but I could see in her blank expression that this gesture was what she thought she was supposed to do when faced with a hysterical person, and there was no tenderness in it. I couldn't stand that. I slapped her hand away. Then the dam broke.

She charged forward, this time with determination. She was strong and pushed me back. I gave way and started to panic. We were just a few feet in front of the shrine when I hit her in the mouth—not with all my strength, but with enough force for her head to jolt back and her lip to discolor. She touched her mouth. No cut appeared. I looked at my red knuckles. I sank down to my knees, more ashamed than I'd ever been in my life. I'd hit my love and she was pregnant.

I grabbed her hand and kissed its heel twice before she jerked it away. She looked at me condescendingly. I'd never hit anyone or anything before; I'd have rather hit myself a thousand times in the face than a person or an animal. I didn't know violence was in my nature. I said "I'm so sorry" again and again but Elodie didn't attend. She walked past me towards the mountain. I let her go. Why not permit the final hammer blow? Everything I thought I was turned out to be wrong.

Elodie investigated the shrine. I expected her to sigh or laugh or cry out in fury or surprise—but no. Silence. After a few minutes that felt like hours she walked past me. She turned slightly, cocked her head, and said, "We're moving to Atlanta. In two weeks. Silas has been offered an important job in something or other. I'll do fieldwork for the Emory anthropology department and volunteer at New Echota on the weekends. It's over. I'm sorry for you. You aren't right. Goodbye."

In the distance, a car engine revved. I sat at the shrine the entire day on my knees, my hands clenching a carpet of moss. The shadow of Devil's Lozenge grew over me. The sun set. Dad came up with a lantern. I didn't move. He kissed my forehead. "Ups-a-daisy," he said, his German accent flaring across that clunky word. "Let's go home. *Alles gut.*" We wove back through the woods arm in arm. Only later did I realize that was the first time in years he'd spoken German to me.

Dad came in and out of my room that night, checking on and taking care of me. I don't think he slept at all. At some point, maybe two or three days later, I awoke without him by my side. I heard snoring in the living room; he was probably asleep in the rocking chair. Sweaty hair was plastered all over my face and I stank horribly. The drowsy, yolky light suggested it was mid-afternoon, maybe three o'clock. All of a sudden, as I walked into the kitchen, intending to refill a glass of water that I'd just gulped down, a thought froze my mind. Dad had found me by the shrine. Had he gone back to investigate it? Had he seen what was inside? Had he found the dolls I'd stolen from his closet? I tiptoed into his room. The boards creaked but he continued to snore. His bed was made up neatly with his favorite quilt covered with owls wearing reading glasses. I snuck into the doll closet, rummaged through the dresses and curls of fake and real hair. A doll with a lace bonnet and pink ribbon around her neck watched me with glass eyes, as did a bearded satyr. In my state of mind they scared me like never before. They were judges. To my even greater despair, behind the careful arrangement of dolls I found the two weathered cornhusk dolls. One showed a faint red stain along its lips and the other wore its black mustache and Panama hat. Dad must've found those accessories in my tackle box. I wept like I've never wept before or since. That doubled the shame after the events with Elodie—that broke me.

I had to leave. I couldn't take it. I retrieved a rucksack from my room, squashed beneath gardening books and threadbare quilts. I threw a few things into it. Some spare clothes. A small umbrella and a canteen. A wool blanket. I went into the kitchen and took out a loaf of bread. It was enough. I didn't have more time since Dad could have woken up from his nap at any moment. I changed into some knickers and a blouse and put on my boots. I pushed open the screen door expertly so that it didn't creak. I tiptoed past the house. I filled my canteen at the pump, and when I neared the garden I sprinted. I ran through the forest, past Quartz Dwarf Falls where the water cascades smoothly down the rock without ever jumping away from it, skirted within a hundred yards of the Elodie shrine but not close enough to see it, and scrambled up the steep curve of the Devil's Lozenge spur, with its pockmarked, dimpled rocks and islands of reindeer moss.

I passed through a dark alpine forest carpeted with sprays of green ground cedar and ground pine and climbed the summit rock. Cumulus clouds blew over the sun, darkening the sky then making the light bloom. Atop this minor summit I'd officially left Amelia's World. It was a symbolic place I came to from time to time. The journey downwards was more precarious, but I made it to a hollow where old-growth oaks and hickories flourished. After fording a clear, cold, swift-running creek, I came to a forest service road. I knew exactly where I was. And it occurred to me where I was going, where I had to go—Granite City. That was the place to hide, to nurse my shame in the dark, to live for a week or die in the shallow caverns where, in days gone by, a hermit dwelled.

High narrow walls of disintegrating granite, with passages never more than two feet across, spider-webbed across the mountainside, creating a maze that forced one to shuffle sideways. I'd gotten lost there a dozen times. Within the dark, branching fissures, mossy and always dripping with water, the sun never showed its full face. Golden brooks flowed beneath the boulders, and snowbanks, stained with red and purple algae, undulated alongside the brooks. Down there, vestiges of snow lasted throughout the entirety of summer, even in warm years.

Into Granite City's maze I went. I slipped through the cracks, turned left, right, left, plunged downwards, then upwards, until I wasn't sure where I was anymore. I scrambled into a pocket of darkness. It was relatively dry there. A broken brass lantern lay deeper down in the recess, along a last rim of light before total darkness, as did a few glass jars, still intact, and a deflated, rusty wheel. I took out my blanket and curled up against the wall. I almost wanted a demon hermit, chewing his beard with shark teeth, to crawl out of the depths and devour me. Anything to cool the heat of this misery and shame. I didn't want to live anymore. I'd failed everyone.

Thunderstorms passed through Granite City, but I only got a little wet in my cave of choice; while the rain rushed under the boulders, I just felt slightly damp. I ate handfuls of bread. After the second day the bread was so hard I had to break it on a rock to get at the slightly softer insides. Salamanders hid under visors of stone and colonies of camel crickets wandered in unison up and down the fissures. I dreamt of Elodie: the feel of her nipples; the lushness of her armpit hair and its bittersweet, acrid stink; her birthmark, the tiny, crushed bird I'd never again squeeze between my fingers; her kitchen that smelled of spices and imported teas; the summer drives in her Ford; her cute and annoying history lessons; the faraway look on her face when she told me goodbye.

I thought of Dad. How worried he must be. How I'd lied to him and he'd found out my lie. How I couldn't confront him. I couldn't think logically about consequences. Shame trapped me in a spinning cage. Hunger scraped at my stomach like a debarking tool. I played the scene between me and Elodie a thousand times. The punch. The words I'd used towards her that she'd never forgive. I hated myself. I struck the back of my head against the wall. I blacked out for a second, then couldn't get my thoughts straight for many hours, not until I'd had a few long naps. The canteen refreshed me and I scooped up fresh water from beneath the boulders.

At times I heard distant shouts and shook with fear, thinking once or twice, due to the twitch of shadows, that someone was repelling down into the grotto. At night grating noises came from the recesses of the cave, perhaps the ghost of a hermit sharpening tools. A blob of sunlight hung loosely on the outside rocks like a turkey wattle. A black speck above the light expanded into a roving black eye. Moss sprouted from a hole in the rock, forming a green watery beard that flowed across the boulders and inundated me. Tiny moons floated across the darkness. The broken brass lantern spoke with a tongue of flame, calling me "worthless and violent." Despite these hallucinations, I'd always come back, gasping and breaking through reality's surface, the memories of Elodie painful enough to run a hook through my cheek and keep me half-sane.

I played the anchoress in that cave for five days before the search party found me. Dad led the way, sidling through the narrow passageway, his glasses askew, his hair wild, and his eyes sleepless, bloodshot, desperate. He called out to me. I couldn't do anything but respond, weakly, to his call. He rushed upon me, heaving. I rested my chin on his shoulder. I expected to feel the angular nudge of a camera, but Dad didn't seem to have one with him for once.

Men in overalls, hunting shirts, and even one wearing a black suit and tie filtered in behind him. Two, five, ten men. An old-timer named Lum with a jutting straw-colored beard. Two young men I didn't know, probably brothers, wearing felt hats. Millsap, the preacher, who was scraped up and dirty, being a bit too large a man to glide through the fissures without experiencing some painful squeezes. Hollis Turpin, the prominent farmer, whose cows famously nursed his pigs. The younger men in the group clapped and smiled while the older men examined me severely.

I wanted to die when I thought about that sleepless search for me across the mountains, forests, rivers, and remote forest roads that had taken place since my departure. A whole community, and some people I'd never met before, would think of me ever after as the hare-brained runaway. They'd marshaled a grand effort, expended resources and care, all for me. And for what? What had my fleeing from home accomplished? If I only could have melted into the streams below the rocks. Disappeared into another, greener world. That would've been nice. I wasn't in a state to note everything accurately. But I swear I heard the phrase "Elodie's girl," and some of the men gave me ironic looks that implied private sequences playing out in their heads. I wanted them to vanish into thin air, but they stubbornly remained, waiting for the scene of reunion to end.

They supported Dad, wobbly with emotion, and insisted on carrying me home in a stretcher that materialized out of nowhere. The words "wayward" and "odd" were whispered. Whether they referred to my affair with Elodie or this senseless adventure I didn't care; it was probably both. Dad was so tired, so senseless, and so happy to have found me that he didn't seem to hear these whisperings.

I convalesced, of course. I didn't leave our property for another fifty years. I guessed at the rumors, but no one ever tried to harm or interfere with me. The preacher didn't condemn me at the pulpit. I drifted out of sight, almost out of the town's memory, just like Elodie, whom I never heard from again. A thousand times I dreamed of writing her letters, of chasing her through a thousand landscapes. Over time, my solitude became less about fear, shame, and grief than a pleasant habit. The life of a hermit suited me: gardening and wandering the well-known forest, relishing the details of Amelia's World, bronze fennel, persimmon trees, stray boulders, the smooth cascade, and Devil's Lozenge like a thunderhead crashed into the earth.

None of Dad's visitors ever mentioned Elodie in my presence, until a photographer acquaintance from Judaculla stayed over in 1962 and mentioned that his second cousin's wife, Elodie McWaters Fenton, who used to live around here, had died suddenly in Atlanta. She was a firecracker, he said.

Woolgathering

As I hobbled down Main Street towards home, I had to struggle to remember why I'd come to Attic Window in the first place, and why I'd allowed the strange Scotsman into my life. My spine curled at the top like a ghost plant, and it ached with each step. I sucked on my burnt finger.

All the while I maintained my distance from Sir Walter, who jabbed his walking stick into the pavement a hundred feet ahead of me. I followed him, making sure to walk more slowly than he did. Eventually he formed a tiny snail's horn on the hilltop. He did not glance back at me as he limped along; he hesitated for a moment, then made his way to the right, up 4th Street towards Walhalla, South Carolina. Cloudily, as through dark stained glass, I saw his thin hair lift and his clothes ruffle before he vanished behind the building that used to be Bob's Soda Shop in days gone by.

His vanishing filled me with relief. I might've even experienced joy if an angel descended and whispered in my ear that he was dead. The sudden transformation in his expression as he'd stood over my collapsed body haunted me. I didn't fear him physically. I favored myself in a contest of strength if it came to that. But some twig had clearly snapped in his brain. His eyes had blazed and bulged in a way I now found darkly comical, his white hair awry, his antique clothes sweat-logged, dripping like icicles in the sun; even his trouser legs were soaked as if he'd peed himself. He'd propelled me to visit Attic Window and now I didn't need him.

But this shimmering barrier behind me—I turned around to catch a last glimpse of it before moving on. It was beautiful and terrible. Did it enclose my slice of Appalachia? If that was the case, was I trapped inside it with Sir Walter? Stranded here with him? And what would he do now? Could he survive without me, in a new ecosystem that he had no knowledge of (could he even survive on his own in Scotland, without a maid and a cook to supply his needs)? The grocery store was well stocked. Would he really leave me alone or would he sneak up on me in the night and do mischief? This anxiety, added to my exhaustion and pain, made me feel a hundred years old. It took me at least ten minutes to walk the tenth of a mile to town center. All the while the extraordinary woman on horseback paced through my mind with bells jingling.

The wild, gamy wind blowing from the direction of Icecandle Mountain whooshed, and as I crossed 4th Street, the gusts, warm as though originating deep inside lungs, broke into ropes, lashing and nearly knocking me over. It forced me to walk at an angle, no matter how hard I tried to barrel straight ahead. I glanced quickly, nervously, to the right, thinking I might see Sir Walter walking up the road or collapsed on the sidewalk. But no. I nearly rammed into the brick wall of what used to be an old hotel and was now a furniture boutique. When I made it to the other side, and was out of the crosshairs of 4th Street, the wind abruptly died.

As I proceeded down the mountain, sunlight, a mixture of honey and motor oil, spilled across the landscape. Dad's message echoed in my mind: "Almost there. The harvest sun. Look up. The gauntlet nearly run." The muted, spotted sun (rather than the eclipsed one) inhabited the sky on this side of the mountain. I looked up, as Dad had written. I'd never heard of the harvest sun before. My guess is that this gauntlet, this series of trials and encounters, will end up there, in the harvest sun, in reunion or oblivion. But if the sun is my destination, by what means will I get there?

My knees creaked audibly by the time I passed my mailbox and opened my screen door. I half expected to see a broom laid across my threshold since, in old folktales, witches can't cross them, but luckily Sir Walter and his delusions had not invaded my home. I collapsed on the rocking chair, not having the energy to make it all the way to bed. I sank into oblivion, and day turned to night, and night to day, and I awoke, imagining I'd heard the plaintive call of a mourning dove. I sat bolt upright, listening intently, since I'd heard no birds for a long time. The call, however, didn't recur.

I went over to the window, afraid Sir Walter, now a madman, awaited me in the yard or sat amidst the stubble of my fallow garden, yet he wasn't there—just the wilting cornstalks, the browning vines, the rusted water pump, and the clotheslines. I waited. Still no movement outside.

My head ached; my skull's sutures shifted like tectonic plates. I feared that I, like Sir Walter, would lose my mind, and that fear (if that makes any sense) scared me, because I hadn't dreaded going insane since I returned home in the aftermath of the Elodie debacle. Back then, I was bedridden for a year, ever on the brink of mental collapse. But I'd never let that happen again. I mustered my courage. I cleaned myself and crawled over to my bed, climbed up precariously, interlocked my fingers, and followed my breath, in and out. Gradually the mental static evaporated.

I'm quite sure that the dream I had was epic in nature, but I can only remember a few scenes from it, centering on the mysterious woman on horseback. Unlike my dreams of Elodie, who always runs from me, the woman on horseback came towards me eagerly when I desired her, the horse's bells tinkling. At one point I rode behind her, holding on to her bare hips for dear life, and despite my fear of falling from the horse, I felt wetter and more ravenous and hot-blooded than I'd ever felt as a young woman. Her wild hair that smelled of honeysuckle flared and tickled my face; the reek of her armpits was so bitter and familiar I nearly swooned. We galloped towards a cliff face. I begged her to stop, but she wouldn't, and I braced to hit rock. Instead we leapt through it and entered an entirely new landscape of buttes, mesas, and tablelands. Nothing but desert to the horizon's end (I've never been west of North Carolina, but I've seen photographs of those eerie sandstone landscapes). A figure galloped towards us, a speck that grew until another mounted rider came into view: a woman with mica skin and antlers on her head.

In another part of the dream, the mysterious woman wore a silver breastplate, gauntlets, and greaves. I was her wife. We lived in a thatched cottage, like those I've read about in fairy tales where candle flames throw gold coins onto the windowpanes. She opened the cottage door into one big open room. I pretended to be asleep on a narrow bed by the window, with a book resting on my chest. She quietly took off her pieces of armor and lay down naked beside me. She removed the book from my inert fingers and then disappeared under the covers. I began to giggle and gripped her hair like a saddle horn.

I awoke craving mulberries, of bursting their sweet, red-purple fly eyes against my palate. I had a jar of mulberry jam in the cellar. With enormous effort I lugged my sore body out the front door and around the house, opened the squeaky, flaking cellar door, and descended into the semi-darkness. Halfway down the concrete stairs, sunk deep in the musty, earthy underground smell, I realized Sir Walter could be down there. I darted my eyes back and forth. I called his name. What was that shadow hunkering down in the corner? Nothing—just sacks of potatoes. The cellar was a small space. There was nowhere he could hide behind the shelves, well stocked with jars and crates of fruits and vegetables. When I reached the bottom of the stairs, I knocked my elbow and an ear-splitting noise followed that almost made me jump out of my skin; it was just an old broom that had fallen over a washing pan. I found the jar I required and quickly ascended the stairs. I kicked myself for not having locked the front door, but upon an examination of my house, no one seemed to have entered; there were no muddy boot prints, nobody inside the closets or under the beds. I resolved to be more careful in the future. For all I knew, in this fractured state of things Sir Walter was, in fact, the warlock and could enter through my chimney.

I feasted on mulberry jam spread on carrots (a delicacy unique to me, as far as I know), and the next morning I had more energy, felt less achy and ancient. I had the luxury to find myself rather bored. Part of me wanted all this madness to be over, but the other part felt more alive than I had in years. It wasn't possible to understand what was happening rationally. No amount of mental work could accomplish it. If this was my apocalypse, or mine and Sir Walter's, or the consequences of Dad's fear of death and turn to Mary-worship, I could accept it and anchor myself in the present.

I bandaged my burnt finger, spent the early afternoon rounding out the story of Elodie and me on the blank pages I'd left for it in this journal, and decided to take a tour of Amelia's World. I'd been so focused on exploring Hemlock Cove that I hadn't visited my usual haunts in some days; doing so always grounded me. I passed the water pump, my large, beloved, fallow garden fenced with chicken wire, and ventured down the hill and across Quartz Dwarf Creek, past the cascade with the pool I used to slide down as a girl and bruise my heels; the same pool where the petrified cloud found its resting place. I took off my shoes and waded into the pool but, as usual, the rocks looked almost identical. I then entered the hardwood forest. At first I thought I'd head east to the ivy-covered chimney, which I loved to climb up and peer into, imagining that it offered a view of another world, a dark subterranean Elsewhere that I could never access. In the end, however, I determined that the old shrine below Devil's Lozenge suited my mood better.

As I passed my autumnal friends, I said hello to each of them: lady fern, ghost plant, blue wood aster, goldenrod, striped gentian, and Indian cucumber root with its lonely dark berry. Everything was goldening. I skirted around the derelict cemetery that always scared me as a child and that Dad called a sacred place, surmising that two underground waterways met directly beneath it (he never produced any evidence for this belief and I've never detected the sound of running water, but given my uncanny experiences at this place, it wouldn't surprise me if it actually was an elemental crossroads). At last I came to the boulder-field at the foot of Devil's Lozenge. It had been many years since I'd investigated the alcove in the mountain where I'd made the shrine to Elodie. The place had stopped stirring bitter shame long ago. I still avoided it, however.

Inside it a pair of photographs lay on a patch of moss. I snatched them up. They were worn at the edges and discolored. Yet the subjects were not in doubt—Elodie and me, sometime in 1926, sitting together on a buck-rail fence with Icecandle Mountain looming in the background. The photographs were duplicates, but one showed both our laughing faces, and in the other, eerily, Elodie's face had been burnt out, as if a cigarette had been pressed to it. In one, Elodie flashed her teeth, eyes squinting playfully at the camera; in the other, a burnt hole hovered above her pearl necklace and brocade dress. In both images I was laughing, head tilted to the side and eyes downcast, seemingly gazing at Elodie's bare arm.

On the back of the photographs I recognized Dad's handwriting; he'd scribbled: "Which one?"

I'd entirely forgotten that this photograph had ever been taken. Elodie and I had been picnicking on Bald Rock and, on the way back, randomly ran into Dad photographing the ramshackle red farmhouse under the Icecandle cliffs. I had no copies of this picture at home. Recalling how Dad had left photographs around the property towards the end of his life for me to collect and comment upon, it wasn't too strange to come across this pair of prints. The riddle on the back, however, and the burnt-out face of Elodie, was not only unnerving but offensive, invasive. As a younger man, before his illness, he would've never pulled this kind of stunt and risked my fury.

Despite myself, I contemplated his question: "Which one?" What was Elodie to me now? A set of memories to be repressed, effaced, or something to accept and even look back upon with graciousness and self-forgiveness? The latter option felt closer to my heart, but I did not want to choose, especially at this prompting from another person, even if it was Dad. Both photographs could coexist within me, though I didn't want to possess either of them physically. So I gathered dead leaves and piled them in the niche, burying the photographs three inches deep. Never would I uncover them. They could decay here over the years, all alone, without my interference. A song by one of those rock-n-roll groups I'd heard a couple times on the radio and listened to from beginning to end—such a rarity for me— came to mind. "Let it be, yeah, let it be, whisper words of wisdom, let it be."

One of Dad's younger friends, Gretel Womack I believe her name was, would often sing that song to herself softly: "When I find myself in times of trouble, Mother Mary comes to me, speaking words of wisdom, let it be." One evening, while Gretel was reading a fable aloud to Dad called "The Wasp and the Butterfly," maybe sometime in 1976, Gretel said that, in her opinion, the moral of the story was to "let it be and live in the present." She sang the first stanza of that song by the rock-n-roll band and, from the kitchen, I sang along with her. We both laughed as we sang, but she didn't come to me and I never joined them in the living room that evening.

Bear Shadow City

After leaving the alcove in the cliff, I forgave Dad his invasive little metaphor. In my heart I knew he meant well, and besides, it was another message from him beyond the grave. I remembered then the boxes of his photographs that had initiated my adventures. I cut across the woods towards Dad's workshop. "The gauntlet nearly run"—surely I'd discovered most of the secrets in the Hemlock Cove region, and maybe only a couple more photographs would provide the maps I needed to find the rest. A cold wind blew from the west. I shivered. Branches clawed the sky. The wind blew again, but it was a different, warmer wind, coming from the north. Did I detect that wild, gamy scent of fresh roadkill and crushed flowers? Luckily I'd put on my wool coat before leaving the house; the weather was changing for the worse. I entered Dad's archive (an apt word, since it was no longer a living, breathing workshop, only a place for recollection). Wind slipped through a broken pane, and again I detected the scent that had earlier been confined to the corridor of 4th Street. What was it? And why had it become so pervasive? It came from the direction of Icecandle Mountain. Thinking of that grandmother of mountains, with its granite buttresses and falcons swooping over wind-flattened shrubs, I located a box of Dad's labeled "Mountains." I flipped through the blue folders until I came to a tab labeled "Icecandle."

Dad had taken photographs of the mountain from every angle possible, from Grimshawe to Bearpen Road, from the northern cliffs to the summit. They were all sepia-colored and smoky, with the crowns of pines and hemlocks sharply etched in the distances. Cloud shadows stained the cliffs black. One photo in particular arrested me; it was the only color, or rather technicolor, image in the lot. Taken from a pull-off, it showed the mountain's shadow in late autumn or early winter, when it formed, quite precisely, the shape of a black bear on the hills below. It looked like the bear was swimming across a choppy red and yellow lake. Elodie, I remembered, had once talked to me about the sacred bear of the Cherokee, the *Yonah*; many times she'd driven with Silas or a woman friend to the roadside overlook to marvel at its shadow, though never with me.

Once again I felt that old tug of curiosity. What was Ice-candle Mountain like now? The same after all these years? Was it the final gateway that would lead to Dad's soul? Did it have anything to do with this strange, warm wind? Could I possibly glimpse that beautiful woman on horseback again? Had Sir Walter gone there? That thought made me shudder. But no, he'd gone down the road towards South Carolina. It was possible he'd encountered another shimmering barrier and been forced to come back, but maybe he was able to keep going; maybe he'd continue on past the Blue Ridge, the Piedmont, the Coastal Plain, and end up on the Atlantic Ocean's white sands, where, if people still existed, and ships still plied the waves, he could sail back to his homeland.

Dad would've acted differently towards Sir Walter, I'm sure of it. He would've fawned over him, asked him to read aloud passages from *Guy Mannering* and asked about his famous acquaintances in England and Europe; he would've talked with him about his translations of German literature; he would've sat him down on the porch's rocking chair and taken a series of portraits. Sir Walter would've posed in the garden, by the creek, at a writing desk in the lamplight smoking a pipe. Dad would've begged him to stay and talk for days. He certainly would have gotten Sir Walter to sign the frontispiece of our rare first edition of *The Antiquary*.

Thinking of the Scotsman made me uneasy, restless. It was time to leave again, come what may. I needed to see Icecandle Mountain and discover the source of the wind.

I mined my memory for a solution to the problem of getting to Icecandle, eleven miles away. Sir Walter and I hadn't located the keys to the snowbirds' Oldsmobile. Then I thought of sick, angry Alvert Hastie and his trailer, whose plastic windows were curtained with Confederate flags and who worked on old cars as a hobby. I might be able to swipe a key to one of his antiques. I hadn't heard any movement inside when I stopped by on the way to Oldcastle Quarry and had no reason to believe he'd suddenly reappear, gesturing with his gun, demanding that I get off his property unless I'd be willing to do him a favor like mow his lawn for free or pick up some white lightning from the shiner called Pilgrim.

It hurt my feet and made me dizzy to walk the mile to Alvert's trailer. When I got there, I checked the Dodges and Plymouths parked next to the uninhabited goat pen. I had no luck finding any keys. His front door happened to be unlocked, and as with everyone else, it seemed that Alvert had been spirited away. I rummaged through the greasy, moldy dishes on his kitchen counter, thrust my hand into the creases of his cigarette-burnt velveteen sofa, lifted my shirt over my face while I dug out mildewed clothes from under his bed, and came across bullets, a Confederate States half dollar, and a hundred or more Indian Head pennies in a jewelry box. I was about to call it quits when I noticed a birdhouse gourd with a round hole in it, hanging from a nail; the hole was stuffed with silver. Upon closer inspection, the gourd turned out to be Alvert's key nest. I tried all the keys and eventually got a blue sedan to start up. The interior smelled like a wet dog. There was gas in the tank but I couldn't turn on the radio. Although the knobs, gauges, and throttle didn't work like the Fords I'd driven, eventually I figured it out and got the thing chugging along, and very slowly moved towards Attic Window and Icecandle Mountain.

The wheel turned heavily. Driving was pure anxiety. After an absurdly long time, I entered Attic Window and turned right onto 4th Street and crept at ten miles an hour towards Icecandle Mountain, which rose above the trees, its sides undulating like blown glass. A pine tree grew here and there on its buttresses, but mostly you'd think a god had taken an eraser and scratched out the trees from the mountainside, leaving behind a chain of streaked cliffs. All the while the wind gusted more fiercely, rocking the car, with the gamy smell nauseating me.

Icecandle was where Elodie and I had first kissed and where, in many ways, the story of my adult life began. After leaving that mountain everything changed. If I had never kissed Elodie on that summit, would I have gone to college, married, moved to Asheville or Michigan or Oregon? Would that have been better? Would my life have felt richer if I hadn't become the eccentric crone with nothing but a father's love and troubled friendship? Somehow, I doubt if I would have been happier, seeking out larger joys instead of the subtler ones of garden and forest.

I parked on Wildcat Road. I could hardly open the door due to the wind's pressure. I walked to the overlook, hugging my coat close to my body as the wind gusted over me. Late October is just the right time of year for Icecandle Mountain to cast its bear-like shadow; and as I approached the guardrail there it was. But something more as well: the bear shadow was not just a shadow anymore; it had volume and dimension. It was breathing, inflating and deflating, and creating the wind that ripped through the valley. Between the gasps issuing from the giant bear's mouth came calls, cries, and bellows. Whenever the shadow didn't breathe, I heard them.

I had not felt the absence of the animals from this region very much. Dad and Elodie had taken up too much of my mind, and the wonders emerging around me made me less conscious of them than I normally would be. Sir Walter, stranded on this side of the ocean and time, had felt it more keenly; he'd addressed it on a few occasions. Poor, mad Sir Walter.

Now I missed the animals, too. I'd had a cat once. She died on the porch's rocking chair while I was out gardening. She was alone. Dad was off taking photographs. For many years, whenever I thought of that beautiful, sweet Abyssinian cat with the amber and black fur and raccoon tail, my eyes swam. Thinking of her, of Moida, but also of the pleasures of new experiences and living dangerously, I decided to find out what creatures cried inside the shadow.

There was no way to drive down to the mountain's foot. I had to buck up and walk down to it. I found a walking stick to help me; I wasn't so different from Sir Walter now. I descended a lower spur of the massif, with the wind forcing me to catch hold of rhododendron branches.

The shadow's breath paused. An animal bugled. Another yelled. Still others tweeted, mewed, and bleated. It was like approaching a circle of hell with all that ruckus. But the noises didn't seem agonized; perhaps a little desperate, angry, or longing for a mate or companion. Only the wind coming from the shadow's mouth sounded labored and almost wheezy, making my ears tingle.

At last the slope leveled out and I spied the shadow's verge. I leapt, somewhat clumsily, over a furious little creek and then came to a place where a witch hazel and hemlock tree stood side by side. Twigs flew against my face. I looked around, confused. Had a branch or pinecone just dropped from above? An object whizzed near my shins and took a triple bounce and vanished into the leaves.

Someone was throwing rocks at me. I ducked under the witch hazel tree, making myself as small as possible, shielding my body with my walking stick. Through a latticework of branches, I saw a human. A man. Another rock flew above my head. In a crouching posture, with an arm across his leg like he'd just thrown a pitch, I glimpsed Sir Walter, breathing heavily.

"Aha!" he called. It was difficult to hear him over all the discord in the great shadow.

"Fucking bastard," I cried, truly incensed. "Don't do that again. I swear that…"

"Silence! Stop your pattering! I know what you've done to me. I would've never believed it before; my mind was too judicious! But I've seen it with my own eyes. Send me back! You've summoned me like a djinni. Have you no heart? I was on my deathbed, for Christ's sake. But you cast your spell, conjured a soul weak from protracted illness and old age, no longer a writer, ready to meet my wife and dogs again in the paradise beyond this sublunary prison. What I once thought superstition and absurdity cannot be so! My faculties have not failed me; I am alert. By the Divine Power, I know you as a witch, as a reincarnation or confederate of the White Lady of Avenel. And I—I am a Witchfinder. To think, after my long investigations, to join a profession I once scorned. But…you are a witch, you must be! Otherwise you would not have arrived at this charmed spot, between a hemlock, a tree long known to be a favorite for witch's brooms, and a witch hazel. 'Tis all the proof I need after those boxes revealed your true nature. Send me back! Or a miracle save me!"

He picked up a rock from a cairn and threw it. He missed the mark and nearly fell onto his pile of missiles. He recovered, then threw yet another rock. It struck my walking stick and ricocheted.

"Either release me or…I'll murder you! I have no pistol or silver bullet, but I'll find a way. And if your death does not return me to Scotland, at least I have found a small recompense, a haven, near these gentle beasts, that you, surely, have trapped in yon globe of darkness."

"I don't think that's why they're called witch hazels! I think the term comes from…"

"Pshaw, pshaw! Wily hag! Double-faced jade! Viper! Hold your tongue! I won't hear more. A palsy on the fair sex if the fair sex means you!" He clutched his head and moaned. "Oh, my God! God Almighty help me through this crucible. Strengthen me. By and by, with or without you, I'll do what I must! These times are not like the old ones. I'd have never come to this pass in Scotland!"

"Just stop," I called, a little more evenly. "I haven't trapped you here. I know you're scared. I don't know what's going on either." He didn't reply. I tried to change tack and pacify him with normal conversation. "I saw you go the other direction on the road. How did you end up back here?"

"I was beckoned here by the wind. By the breath. Who couldn't be? Your snare, if it be that, worked a charm. But don't attempt to lull me into inaction. How else could these fantastic events have occurred? I'm not such a fool and knave. I've lived long enough to know an uncanny wench when I see one. I snap the wand of peace on my knee. I shall dispatch you with the utmost celerity!"

"You're not thinking straight. I'm thankful that you helped me, but remember that I helped you, too. I'm going to come over to you now. Don't throw a rock at me. We're both too old for this nonsense."

I half stood up and advanced a step. Sir Walter didn't reach for a rock. I raised myself to my full height and took another step. I glimpsed a stockpile of odds and ends near his cairn: a makeshift knapsack, a water gourd, a coat, and his walking stick. He looked like a wandering beggar; his hair was disheveled and his trousers, shirt, and white beard were smeared with either dirt or excrement. I crept forward, telling him it would be fine, that I would not hurt him, that I wasn't a witch, but would help him as much as I could; that I'd find a house for him somewhere in town where he could live out the rest of his life in peace and quiet. When I came to within a yard of him, he snapped out of his trance and lunged for a rock. He was too slow; before he could even draw the rock behind his head—an act that a young person could've accomplished in a third of the time—I pushed him over. The rock flew out of his hand. He fell like a scarecrow with its pole uprooted. He moaned. He spouted expletives, half of which I couldn't understand.

"Stay put," I told him. I put my foot on his chest. "What's over there in that shadow? What's moving inside it? Did you look?"

"If you won't send me back to Abbotsford, at least find my poor dogs in there. I wanted to enter it but was repelled by a buck with thirty tynes…" He started to cry and talk incoherently. I couldn't get much else out of him that I could mentally translate to English, except for "accursed yowling," "nombles and raven bones," and "the bounties of Morpheus." I scanned the area, quickly saw what I wanted, and dragged over a fallen pine branch about two arms' width. I laid it across Sir Walter. It was heavy enough to keep his frail body pinned without hurting or suffocating him. I couldn't have him attacking me from behind while I investigated the shadow.

I moved forward, cautiously. Icecandle's cliffs fell from the clouds like petrified, multi-tiered waterfalls. The sun was hidden. The shadow leavened above the trees. Where it began, the trees vanished altogether; the shadow was like the mountain's dark double, huge and substantial in the same way. But unlike the rocky heights above me, the shadow, as my eyes adjusted to its inner cavity, rose and fell, and seemed to contain giant organs, lungs, and muscles, barely distinguishable from the darkness encompassing them. A mountainous bear, part living, part phantom, its stomach sliced open and half gutted—that's the best idea I could form of the place. Yet I wasn't alone in there. As the vast shadow heart beat irregularly at least a thousand feet above me (it was hard to gauge distance), the cries, which had gone quiet when I'd passed the shadow's border, erupted. I turned to run, but bodies, animal bodies, perhaps birds, squirrels, foxes, and opossums, among others, dark garnet like the shadows around them, cobbled into a wall, blocking my exit.

A goat's face appeared inches from my nose, thrust out its dark grey tongue, and yelled. Then a bristly snout, a piglet's snout, maybe, wormed violently into my open mouth, snuffed, and then retreated, leaving a track of dirt along my tongue. I gagged; the dirt tasted sour, mealy.

I couldn't scream. I was too scared. And Sir Walter, since I'd disarmed him, couldn't help me. My heart thumped. I thought I might die of a heart attack if the animals didn't consume me first.

For a moment I got caught between velvety antlers; a deer rolled its black eye and jumped into the semi-darkness, the band on its tail moon-grey rather than white. A squirrel ran up my body as if it were a tree, chirped and chattered in my ear; another ran after it, barking, and they both dug claws into my scalp and flew away. The animals teeming everywhere seemed to give this space substance; they circulated like blood. Figures ran up the walls of the shadow, along veins of night, towards the beating heart that shuddered like an obsidian chandelier in a heavy wind.

The animals drew me in a wave along warm walls of twitching muscle. I had the strong impression that this shadowland served as a kind of depot, a rendezvous point, for all the animals in western North Carolina; animals not just from the present, but from the past and perhaps the future as well: elk, bison, mountain lions, jaguars, and maybe even wooly mammoths and saber-toothed tigers. There were so many of them, such diversity. The smell of fresh, tangy feces, wet hair, and saliva was overpowering.

Buoyed by the animal tide, I was drawn farther from the outside light, entering the shadow's interior. Webs of fat slicked me. I went under the animal current for a moment and panicked, thinking I was going to drown. A dog was suddenly thrust into my arms. It nuzzled its snout into my armpit for protection. I tried to hold it with all my might. It lifted a paw, which rotated in slow drunken circles. I thought of Sir Walter, how happy he'd be if I was spit out of the bear shadow, my arms wrapped around a dog—his dog for all I knew. That might pacify him a bit. I might be able to trust him enough to take him back to Hemlock Cove, and perhaps install him in the Hillipses' house; or even better, convince him to live in a house in Attic Window, across from the grocery store with enough miles between us so that he wouldn't vex me too much. But the dog proved too greasy, and without complaint, it gradually slipped from my arms.

The shadowland continued to hum with activity—yet an inconstant activity, dammed up and deluging, stuttering, the surge of bodies increasing, decreasing, branching, cycling. Somewhere high above me giant lungs pumped and twilit skin expanded and contracted. It took all my willpower and guile to stay above the animal tide. My feet touched down on a surface from time to time, and I sensed I was traveling upwards, riding along a diagonal bone speckled with flesh, little bumps of it. Twirling wires of light lashed the darkness, vanished, and forked like copper lightning.

Up ahead, the faint outline of a normal-sized black bear came into view, standing on its hind legs, dancing on the giant bone. It squatted and kicked. It linked arms with an invisible partner and turned in tight circles, narrowly avoiding the bone's edge and arcing back. I was reminded vaguely of some of the dance postures in Dad's favorite painting, William Holbrook Beard's *The Bear Dance*, hanging on the back wall of his workshop. Then the choreography changed. The bear brought its arms down in steady succession, one after another, beating an absent drum. I came to a halt a few feet in front of it, as though placed there by the animals, who receded in a wave back down the bone ramp. The bear rubbed its belly with its forepaws.

As the moments passed inside the living, breathing, seething shadow of Icecandle Mountain, I had to labor to keep my senses sharp, but I had the feeling that I was in the presence of what the Cherokee called a medicine bear, one that could talk and read human minds. I had such scant knowledge of that tradition, unlike Elodie (who certainly would've told me all about the *Yonah*), so I couldn't be sure if that was the right term or the correct judgment.

Suddenly the bear froze. I hadn't realized its eyes were closed until they flared open, revealing amber irises with pupils dancing like will-o'-the-wisps. Those eyes gave off the only rich color in the shadowland. It held out its paw, motioned for me to come forward. Even if I'd wanted to, I couldn't force my limbs to move. The bear took a heavy step towards me. The bone we were standing on vibrated. The blinking, forking light from the outside world, now so far away I doubted I'd ever reach it again, showed me an ancient black bear, its hair dusted with dandruff.

The bear smelled of mold in forgotten coffee cups and the ammonia-like breath of animals with kidney failure. But also like a whiff of honey, barely detectable like pollen blowing in the night. I thought of this creature as the pilot bear inside this giant, wrecked bear ship.

It made a gesture I didn't understand. Its claws curled, inched backwards and forwards. I continued to stand like a tree. A sigh escaped the bear's mouth, as if to say: silly human. It touched my pocket lightly, and traced the outline of the Virgin Mary there, who, over the last weeks, had grown thin, having lost so many of her attributes. I withdrew the figurine hesitantly; I didn't want to give any more of her away. Yet she had to serve her purpose, which I guessed was to act as a key to the harvest sun.

The bear took the Virgin from my hand. Its amber eyes widened when the figurine passed its sharp teeth and disappeared into its gullet. It closed its eyes meditatively. Then the choking began.

The bear coughed. It lifted its paws and touched its throat. It retched, gasped, trying to breathe but unable to capture air. It fell over and rolled onto its stomach. Released from a spell, I ran over to it, clasped my hands under its throat and cinched over and over with my forearms, hoping to eject the figurine from its mouth. The bear gurgled, coughed, then collapsed into rigid stillness.

Its corpse deflated, melting into liquid that ran in waterfalls off the bone's edge. Soon nothing was left of it. I could just make out the Virgin Mary figurine, however, lying in a pool of blood. I snatched her up. I couldn't see what had gone missing from her, not at first, but as I held her up to the west, towards the hidden sun's light, the figurine glinted like metal. The upper part of the wooden casing had been eaten; the Virgin's inner marrow had become a blade of razor-sharp gold. I could tell that it was a blade of power that wouldn't break under the heaviest anvil.

As I marveled and tried to wrap my head around what had just happened, and attempted to map out a possible escape route down the bone, a rustling sound, as of leaves stirring, filled the darkness in front of me. Shadows accumulated like flecks of iron to a magnet that fused into the shape of a bear. A young, healthy bear, its muscles taut under lavish fur, a bear standing on its hind legs and staring at me with bright amber eyes. It nodded. Somehow the old bear, like a phoenix, had melted into nothingness and been reincarnated. It turned its back to me and sat down.

Something, perhaps animals I couldn't see and thought had left the scene, thrust me up onto the bear's back.

Before I could say *no*, or *wait*, the bear jumped off the bone, down five hundred feet or more, snapping the cords of flesh dangling across the shadowland. The bear galloped towards a crosshatch of red-blue evening light. By a miraculous balancing act, it kept me astride its back even though only one of my hands gripped its fur. My other hand wielded the golden Virgin blade, which I couldn't manage to pocket as we careered forward—I was afraid I'd stab myself or the bear. But in that headlong charge, brief moments occurred when I thought I was the bear rather than atop it; that I had somehow merged with it and my soul reveled in a canny wildness.

A big, dark creature, maybe a bison, darted in front of us. The bear evaded it with a graceful sidestep. Birds' wings exploded in my face. Cold fish scales parted around my neck. Near the shadow's opening, which we were already approaching, a grey deer on its back, stock still with its legs spread as in a sex act, seemed to await being trampled down by our fierce progress. We dodged it. I thought I saw the bear thrust out its tongue and lick the deer as we charged past.

I hardly knew what happened on the shadow's margin, but I recall the trace of irony in the bear's look, an irony mingled with warning, as it dumped me onto the leaves, stood on its hind legs for a moment, and reclaimed the shadow. I reached out my arms, for I had lost another precious thing.

The earth turned away from the last red flush on the horizon. Icecandle Mountain loomed above me. Suddenly, accompanied by hissing and popping sounds like a waterfall of pebbles, the great shadow dissipated; the rattling breath vanished, either for good or until tomorrow when the sun hit the mountain at the right angle to create the bear.

Beyond the hills, a milky, gelatinous barrier, the same one I'd encountered at the far end of Attic Window, came into view, shimmering as jellyfish are said to do in the ocean. It rose behind Icecandle Mountain and reached its arms to west and east. A moaning, low-pitched but constant, caught my attention. I crawled towards it in the darkness, sticks stabbing my palms and pinecones pricking them. I called Sir Walter's name.

The moaning continued. I smelled Sir Walter before I touched him; I think he'd had a bowel movement. His leg jerked away. He tried to kick me, I think, but was too weak.

"Are you returned?" Sir Walter cried. "Remove this branch at once! I cannot take the shame any longer. I'll die of it. A duel betwixt us must occur soon. But it's so cold. Oh, for a draught of Usquebaugh!"

A terrible chill struck my bones when he said those words. A frozen eyelash fell on my arm. I swept it off. Then another fell. I waved my hand in the air and encountered big thick snowflakes. They came down with a fury. A wind blasted me, different from the organic stink pumping from the shadow's lungs. Leaves flew helter-skelter. I'd left a flashlight somewhere nearby; probably under the witch hazel tree. I crawled around searching for it as the sky unloaded an entire winter's snow. I was afraid it would cover my flashlight before I could find it, but thankfully my sense of direction proved keen. I had to help Sir Walter up the slope and back to the car before this strong winter storm made the roads impassable.

The List in the Folder Labeled "Cold Weather Scenes"

The List:

Gideon Laney
Olen Selleck
Mae Selleck
Jane Millsap
Julia Smith
Imogene Bascom
Mossie Reynard
George Takeshi
Max Straub
Carolina Willingham
Ravenel McWaters
Blanche McWaters
Geneva McWaters
June Eyrie
Exie Heacock
Silas Fenton
Hollis Turpin
Addie Cotton
Jonathon Diffenderfer
Adelaide Warren
Hoyle Mashburn
Aura Mashburn
Lena Smith
Windle Fowler
Mary Fowler
Evelene Fowler

Madge Fowler
Prior Talley
Anna Pond
Vinetta Norton
Verna Holbrook
Fanny Lusk
Bill Fordham
Emma Loblein
Mary Loblein
Lester Hawkins
Mary Hawkins
Kay Hawkins
Velma Nix
Margaret Nix
Dewy Nix
Davene Boynton
Rebecca Ovel
Alfred Weisbrooker
Nellie Emmons
Buist Rivers
Hiram Ruggles
Wade Henry
Alvert Hastie
Granville Lance
Virginia Lance
Cliff Miller
Caroline Growe
Amanda Ernstein
Gretel Womack

First photograph: 1918
Last photograph: 1977 (Finis)

Witchfinder

Sir Walter, even after I'd removed the pine branch from his body and begged him to follow me up the slope, to retreat to the relative safety of my home, refused obstinately.

"So you haven't brought my dogs?" was all he said.

He felt around for his walking stick, found it, and stood up shakily amid the blizzard. He drifted towards the boundary wall, which shimmered and flared through the snowflakes like pale northern lights. The snow swallowed his threadbare figure. I struggled up the slope. I'd lived in the mountains my whole life, had seen dozens of bad winter storms, but they paled in comparison to this.

I thanked my guardian spirits when I came to Wildcat Road. After just a few minutes of exhausting plodding and slips and falls I found the parked car. Fear shot through me: I was convinced I had dropped the keys somewhere in the snow or in the bear shadow. I sighed with thankfulness when I touched the serrated metal in my back pocket. I started the car and set the golden blade in the passenger seat. The tires spun and the car's trunk trended to the right.

I turned left onto 4th Street. Snow carpeted the windshield, blinding the view. I had to stop the car in another blaze of panic, wondering if it had wipers that worked. But at last I found the switch; the wipers functioned passably well. I fired the ignition and wove precariously down the road. What worried me most was the steep downward descent into Hemlock Cove. And I was right to worry. I made it a good way down, but as I attempted to hug a particularly tight turn and apply the brakes at the right time, the car skidded, screeched, and crunched into a tree. I caught myself before hitting my head on the steering wheel, and though I felt a bit whiplashed it wasn't serious. I grabbed the golden blade and opened the car door, a little dizzily, but recognized up ahead the turnoff to the Hemlock Cove Poplar, only a short distance, maybe a couple hundred yards, from my house. An avalanche unlike any the Appalachians had ever seen would have to boom down from the sky for me not to reach it.

I passed my mailbox and shined the flashlight on the housefront. It looked like the snow was blowing underneath the house, scything into its very foundation. A few feet of powder had already accumulated in a wave against the door. I kicked the snow away and entered. I raised my arms and whooped for joy. Then I recalled the golden blade in my hand and simmered down. The blade was short yet beautifully wrought. The Virgin's mahogany legs and crotch served as the handle; the rest of her upper body was gone, having acted, I suppose, as a sheath for the blade. I set it on the shelf above the sink by the two cornhusk dolls, the relics of my shame.

The pipes in the house would soon freeze. I turned off the water; I could melt snow for drinking water if need be. The snow could bury my house, and as long as I could get air, I'd survive. This snowstorm was somehow familiar, perhaps from old stories about the Fimbulwinter told to me as a child. There was a weight to it. A meaning. I knew it in my bones.

The cold sank its fangs into me, dragged them along my nerves. I put Dad's leather jacket with the mink lining atop my own (Velma Nix, the mink breeder, had presented him with that jacket for some portraits he'd taken of her and her grandchildren). I went outside again, braving the storm, and brought in all the firewood from the shed and dumped it on the floor. I hurried to the cellar, shoving snow from its door. I carried as much food as I could manage into the house. The blizzard only intensified. By the time I made my last trip, I was practically swimming through it.

I collected all the sheets, quilts, and comforters from the chest and wardrobe. I considered trekking out to Dad's workshop to rescue some of his photographs, but it wasn't worth tempting fate.

Nestled in my warren of cotton and linen, I dozed by the fire, woke, saw that the snow had risen about two feet up the window, up to the catch. I stoked and added wood to the fire and dozed again.

This might be the end, I awoke thinking. I looked out the window. The snow fell just as heavily as it had hours before. It obscured the garden and the boulder in the front yard. Despite this, I noticed something strange. Earlier, I'd seen the snow line along the window's catch and the line was still in that exact place, notwithstanding the storm's rage. I rubbed my eyes. I ate a bit, then found my pipe. I puffed bright leaf tobacco with my back to the fire, gazing at the looping flakes.

Hours later the storm raged on, yet the snow line hadn't climbed any higher up the windowpanes. Where was it going? I tried to open the screen door, but a hunk of snow like a white, glittering bull lay against it and it wouldn't budge. I shut the heavy main door, not forgetting to lock it, sealing myself in the relative warmth of the house. God it was cold out there. How was I to occupy my time? By reading? I couldn't retain anything under these circumstances. Reflection? When I started to go down that route, too many unaccountable events and unanswerable questions crowded my brain until it hurt. I shut that switch off. I could go on a scavenger hunt around the house, I supposed. I hadn't visited Dad's bathroom for many weeks. Its commonplaceness would be a balm.

I entered the small tile room. Above the shower was a double-paned window thick with spiderwebs. Brown carpet encased the toilet lid. Framed above the toilet was a photograph of a white waterfall and green pool. I opened his mirrored cabinet. I tinkered with his blue plastic single-blade razors. I picked up the tiny scissors he used to cut his nose and ear hairs. A white film, like toothpaste, covered the blades' edges. Here lay curled two of his hairs, one white, one grey. I unscrewed the top from a glass stopper and sniffed; the smell nearly knocked me out. It was what the locals call whoop-ass, an alcoholic tincture made of mountain mint and other secret ingredients that Dad took daily for his health. A scratched camera lens had been propped up in a corner of the cabinet.

I took the lens to the bedroom, held it up to the grey light, and noticed a fingerprint on it, most likely his. I went around his room with the lens held to my eye like a monocle. I played with it like a little girl. I observed objects in new lights, sometimes sharpened, sometimes slightly warped: the Kodak Brownies, Thorntons, and Polaroid cameras under a thin layer of dust, piled in a box in the corner, reminding me of broken and useless artifacts unearthed at an archaeological dig; the nightstand stacked with a random assortment of books on photography and hardback classics; some brittle, faded German fifty marks; and a pair of hexagonal reading glasses with curled earpieces, one of the lenses threaded with cracks as though it had been stepped on.

Dad's forbidden closet was dark. He only had a few suits, shirts, and trousers in there. New clothes didn't entice him very much, and he didn't have the money to buy them, anyway. He wore the same outfit twice per week. They still smelled like him: muscadine wine, pipe smoke, and old age rot. It permeated his clothes. I wondered if I smelled that way now, too. The plywood closet floor was empty of objects, minus a wire coat hanger. The dolls that had once occupied this space, minus the two cornhusks, I'd buried with him under the poplar tree. I'd piled them on top of him, carefully, and then laid down upon them, using them as a buffer so I wouldn't do anything rash or be tempted to embrace his sore-riddled skin.

Looking at the floor of the closet, I noticed a crack. At first it appeared to be a trick of the dim closet light, but there truly was a crack in the wood, surrounded by a perimeter of darkness, as though a black marker had, starting at the wall, drawn a rectangle.

I bent down to investigate the crack. I hadn't noticed such a thing before. Until very recently, however, dolls had occupied the space above it, so that wasn't a surprise. I traced it with my fingers, detected a slight crease in the wood, and tried to pry it open but couldn't manage it. The ruler on Dad's nightstand proved too thick. I went to the kitchen, looking here and there for a suitable tool. Snow zigzagged outside. The remnant of the Virgin Mary figurine, with the rich mahogany handle and golden blade, reflected just enough light to attract me with its brilliancy.

I wedged the golden blade in the crack and pressed down. A click, like a trap, and the crack widened. My stomach muscles twisted. I feared I'd discover a secret down here that would change my view of Dad forever, that would tarnish his memory and make it harder, for all the wrong reasons, to move past his death. Upon applying further pressure, a trapdoor swung gently upwards. A ladder descended into the darkness.

With my flashlight, I descended the strong, soundless wooden rungs. Somehow I knew this place. My room was just across the wall. I'd never heard Dad descend these steps. Yet I think I always half knew it was here. His occasional flurried, evasive moods. The knowing glances of his friends.

A light switch came into view. There wasn't any electricity in the house now, but I tried it nonetheless. Impossibly, a lightbulb flickered and sizzled, radiating skin-yellow light on a concrete floor. I stepped down softly. At the bottom, I gazed around the little room, a vacant crypt, a cenotaph, with only a black plastic chair in the center. It's what I imagined an interrogation room might look like. The walls, however, were plastered with colorful wallpaper.

When it dawned on me, I laughed aloud. Dad, my friend, my idol, my past, my fool, is this all the scandal, all the eccentricity you had inside you? Was there nothing darker, more delirious?

Photographs of breasts: women's, men's, androgynous breasts. Was this Dad's and the town's winking secret? Maybe we were really never that close, even in the old days. His life was a fortified castle, and he'd only lowered his drawbridge to show me the battlements, never the inner keep.

The photographs were beautiful, tasteful even, staged carefully with the subject turning to meet the perfect light. Dark nipples, pink nipples. Old bosoms and young bosoms. Never was the subject's face exposed to the camera, unless it was a nursing baby, such as the one of the bonneted child feeding on an exposed breast, faded grass edging the mother's flower gown. I saw a close-up of a breast with dark chest hairs twirling around a grey nipple; a giant, swollen nipple like a doorknob; a joke photograph of a large bosom balancing two china teacups; a voluptuous chest; a flat chest; wrinkles splintering across a breast like mud in a drought; breasts like gourds hanging from a loose rope; an indentation where a nipple should be; two crescent scars amid surgically trimmed conglomerations of flesh; the inflamed teats of a dog or coyote; parallel rows of pig teats; a tiny hand cupping a breast, with milk dripping out like pus from a wound; flaking, chewed nipples; an androgynous pair of breasts, with dime-sized nipples and a collapsed sternum.

I was surprised a community that claimed to be Christian would permit such an eccentricity, but Dad was well loved, and he got a pass sometimes for being a foreigner, while also being accepted as a local treasure—lucky man. I scanned other photographs. There must have been hundreds. I had so many questions, though part of me didn't care and saw it all humorously. None of the photographs could be of my mother, since Dad didn't take up his hobby until after her death. Some of them might have been breasts of his lovers. And with a lightning flash of curiosity, I wondered if he'd ever taken a picture of Elodie's breasts. If so, would I consider that a violation?

As though willing this possibility into existence, I sleuthed out a photograph that resembled Elodie's breasts mightily. I couldn't prove it, of course. Maybe it was just my fancy. Two lovely round breasts, with only slight creases along the edges to mark the beginnings of age; the dark nipples pert, lively, flaring out at slight angles; the areola dancing with tiny bumps. Such Elodie-like breasts. If they were hers, I wouldn't be surprised if she'd asked Dad to take pictures of them rather than the other way around. She would've enjoyed keeping that kind of secret from me.

A camera, a relatively new black boxy Polaroid, sat on the chair in the center of the room. I hadn't noticed it before, but that wasn't too strange, considering all the images of breasts reeling through my brain along with the fact that it was the exact same color as the chair. The camera attracted me now because of its centrality to the room and because it was spotless—not a speck of dust on it. I picked it up and examined it. The lens had been polished. I looked through the crystal-clear viewfinder. The window on the back indicated two frames left in the film. I don't know what exactly spurred me to put the flashlight down, take up the camera, and place its strap around my neck, but I did. Perhaps it was because it didn't seem like an artifact from Dad's life; rather it felt active, relevant, something he'd touched recently and that still functioned beyond him. I decided to save the last two photos until I had an irresistible urge to take them.

I climbed the ladder and closed the trapdoor. The cotton light had dimmed further. I glanced outside. I couldn't understand why the snow hadn't risen any higher. It came down so relentlessly.

Part of me wanted to dig up Dad's grave under the poplar tree, to exhume the dolls piled on top of him to see if their chests had been etched or mutilated like the figurine of the Virgin Mary when I first discovered her. I went over to the back door. The snow made it impossible to open. Attempting to shovel a path through it would be pointless; every time I scraped a layer away, fresh flakes would refill it.

I remembered the two cornhusk dolls on the kitchen shelf—the very ones that I'd stolen and taken to the shrine where I'd worshipped the debris of Elodie's life, the ones Sir Walter had recently commented upon. I hadn't buried them with Dad because they were the only dolls stained by my association with them. Now I wondered if all the dolls were just a cover for Dad's perversity; if they'd acted as a buffer between me and the secrets beneath the trapdoor. But somehow I doubted that. He lavished too much affection on them, treated them like pets. I unbuttoned the suit of the male cornhusk doll with the black mustache. On his chest, where his nipples would be, two deep Xs had been scored. The same two Xs were on the woman doll's chest.

I couldn't love Dad any less. I'm sure he had other secrets, other mysteries. Who doesn't? The only act that might've crossed a line was photographing Elodie's breasts, but it's possible I would've forgiven him. I wish he were here so I could see the fear in his eyes when I asked him about it.

Suddenly the world lurched. The house frame creaked. *I'm having a stroke*, I thought. My life didn't flash before my eyes, exactly, but time stretched like a rubber band. I crawled unsteadily over to my warren of sheets, had the awareness to set the knife and flashlight in a place I could easily locate them, gripped the covers, and closed my eyes.

The heaving sensation didn't stop. It felt like my house was climbing precipitously, a basket carried by a hot air balloon. The floor trembled. Snow continued to fall outside as if nothing was happening. The chimney cascaded dust. It coughed. It groaned. It cried: "Help me die."

My stomach dropped. I knew that voice. Just in case, I grabbed the golden blade.

I hadn't tended the fire in quite some time and it was cold. The room felt like an icebox. Half unwillingly I dragged myself over to the fireplace and held on to the trembling grate. I twisted myself around and peered up. Wedged in the chimney's throat, caught between the smoke shelf and the bricks, was a white-haired scalp and cornflower blue eyes. Soot and ash streaked the jowls. Initially I thought the person, for it was a person, must be dead, given the awkward angle of his head.

Sir Walter looked as if the chimney were giving birth to him and he was caught with his head poking out, dripping water profusely, the chimney no longer having the will to push.

"Miss Amelia, help me die," he said. His voice trembled with the trembling house. "I'm past my allotted term, past everything. It is an agony to live like this, to want to die but to keep on living—unwanted, without a friend in the world, and without the country that made my heart sing. I'm mauled with rheumatism. My skin has chilblains. I'm made of the willow, not the oak anymore. My headaches are bonfires. I know it is a sin, Lord help me, but I came here with the intention to murder you, and I've been punished for it, stuck in a lum—Sir Walter in a lum! The bell is ringing! It can be done by unnatural or natural means—I no longer care if you are a witch or a woman!"

It was hard to process that, amid this earthquake, Sir Walter Scott was stuck in my chimney. The cold was brutal. I needed to restart the fire. An image of Sir Walter burning like a witch at the stake passed through my mind and dissolved. How to get him out? I reached up and tugged his lapels.

"There's no getting me out," he quavered. "As thin as I am, I had to squeeze my body to a bedpost to fit in here. Alas! A stone edge presses deeply into my chest."

I kept tugging. I squeezed his head between my forearm and withered bicep and dropped down to the grate. I got up, squatted, and used all my force to ram his head back up the chimney's throat with my shoulder; he didn't budge that way either. He yelped but did not complain of my rough tactics.

"'Twill not go, however muckle you try. I am not mad, nor drunken—I know what I am asking of you. Have you a hatchet, mattock, shovel, or pickaxe? I beseech you. If chopping does not work, strangle me—wring my neck! Gnaw my bones!"

The sensation of floating upwards had eased, but it continued in a subtler way. The house shook and creaked a little less. I told Sir Walter that I wouldn't help him unless he told me how he got stuck in my chimney in the first place. And quickly. Something was amiss. Accepting my terms, he told me about how, after he'd left me in the snow, he'd encountered the barrier of pale lightning and trekked alongside it until dawn. The barrier's heat had melted the snow along its perimeter, forming a track about twelve feet wide that proved more or less snow-free. For a while he'd followed a woman on horseback, trotting on the opposite side of the barrier. The world across the wall had, he claimed, an entirely different weather, without a cloud in the sky. He'd lost the woman on horseback at some point and, hungry and confused, dreaming of venison, wild fowl, and buttered crabs, strayed from the barrier and, by a miracle or curse, had ended up at the foot of a very high snow hill. After he'd climbed this snow hill, thinking he would perish from cold, he arrived at my house. Finding the door immovable, and snow-locked, he decided to kill me through some other means; the chimney, given his terrible thinness, might be the best option. The snow had mounted so high that clambering onto my roof wasn't that difficult even in his weakened state—only he'd been forced to abandon his beloved walking stick.

My mind had stopped flowing regularly when he spoke of the woman on horseback.

"What did she look like?" I gasped.

"Who? What?"

"The woman on the other side of the barrier."

"Ah…dark hair, wide mouth, a horse with jingling bells. That's all I can remember."

If the situation was relaxed enough to meditate on her, this woman who fascinated me, I would have done it for a long time.

"I don't care one jot about that!" he cried suddenly. "Gall and wormwood, cut me out of this chimney!" Staring at the golden blade near my hand, his eyes aglitter, he heaved, "And use that! Use that! Stick it here—there's enough of my neck visible! Or you can start a fire with me in your lum! I'll scream *please* until you're mad. I'll never give you peace if you won't allow me mine!"

I thought of how I'd punched Elodie and attacked my doppelgänger. Could an act of violence also be one of justice, kindness? This castaway from another time had come to kill me, after all. I didn't hate him. I even loved some of his novels, but I wanted to get rid of him so badly, to be alone or with better company. I felt sorry for him, too. His fate was, perhaps, worse than death.

"Moses killed," he pleaded. "Pilate killed, as did Paul. Yet this is not a killing, but returning me to my natural state. This afterlife is evil. Return me to my deathbed in Abbotsford or to a heavenly afterlife. Not this earth, this hell. Not this suffering, this hurricane of magic. I can abide it no longer. Miss Amelia, if you be not a witch, be my savior, and I will bless thee."

He moved me. I couldn't help it. My inner machinery altered, the tumblers fell into new positions.

"Would you like to hear a passage of your writing?" I asked. "I've always admired your books."

He couldn't help but blush, even upside down, and at his life's end.

"I cannot say," he said, doing his best to affect modesty. "I do not know if that would be a boon or no."

"May I read my favorite chapter to you?"

He assented.

I took down *The Antiquary* from the bookshelf and opened it. The pages were still creamy and crisp. We were always careful with our books.

"I hope you don't mind if I do not read your introduction, or your ending—neither of them ever satisfied me. I always just wanted you to get on with the story. Your endings were so rushed."

I could tell Sir Walter was taken aback. But I couldn't give him everything. I couldn't lie to a dying man.

I began with Chapter XXXI, Steenie's funeral, which I'd seen Dad weeping over many times and over which I'd wept myself, amazed at the power of a writer to make one care so much about a character entirely insignificant to the novel's plot; the chapter started with an epigraph—usually I didn't read these either, but I didn't inform Sir Walter of the fact:

Tell me not of it, friend—when the young weep,
Their tears are luke-warm brine; —from our old eyes
Sorrow falls down like hail-drops of the North,
Chilling the furrows of our wither'd cheeks,
Cold as our hopes, and harden'd as our feeling—
Theirs, as they fall, sink sightless—ours recoil,
Heap the fair plain, and bleaken all before us.

Sir Walter's eyes swelled with tears, which ran down his upside-down forehead, into his hair, and dripped into the fireplace. With trepidation I attempted the Scottish accents. He smiled when I acted out the speeches of ancient Elspeth and Steenie's mother and father. I smiled, too.

When I reached the end, when the Antiquary departs for his solitary walk on the coast, I kissed the sour tear running down Sir Walter's forehead.

"Thank ye," he said. I touched the golden blade to his throat. He nodded, closed his eyes, and smiled.

I thrust. His smile disappeared.

"Du…na…stup," he gurgled.

I cut across his throat. Blood dumped into the hearth, spraying my face, clothes, and the boxy camera around my neck. Skin and muscles split wide open; the Adam's apple ruptured. The gaping wound widened like a toothless mouth and frowned at me as I sawed across and down. I had to use all my strength when I arrived at his spine. He stopped gurgling. The last bit was difficult to reach. I had to yank his head down and rip the remaining skin away. His head fell, struck the grate, and bounced, grazing me with rough beard and rolling over to the rocking chair.

It was a horrific scene. The house polluted, but no crime to solve, no crime committed.

What to do with his head? Could I take it outside? The solution flashed before my mind. I'd take it to Dad's secret basement room. That could be the head's crypt. The rest of Sir Walter could rot in the chimney.

I turned to his decapitated head. To my horror, his cornflower blue eyes flickered from left to right. My heart sank. Were the nerve endings reacting, like a chicken with its head cut off? Or was the poor man not dead even after all that? How cruel this disintegration, this apocalypse, whatever it is. Once again I had to readjust my expectations instead of crumpling into a ball. I had to finish this job for me, for him. I bent down and looked into his eyes and asked, "What's left?"

He blinked. His eyes, glazed and weary as though drugged, rolled upwards.

Intuiting what he wanted, I drove the golden blade into his scalp; it went in slickly, the blade crumbling as I pushed it farther into his head. Gold showered as though I were a blacksmith hammering a half-molten sword. Was it just my imagination or did I hear the mica children's song, "not see, but sing, not see, but sing," echoing in the near distance, beckoning me to the final door?

Sir Walter closed his eyes. His head looked distant, puppet-like, dispossessed.

The Virgin's legs, which had previously been the blade's handle, no longer contained the heft of magic. The little piece of wood was as useless as a solitary chess piece. I threw it into the fireplace.

The sensation of the house rising precipitously returned with a fury. My stomach lurched. The house seemed to jet faster and faster into the ether. I glanced out the window. It had stopped snowing.

Madonna of Carolina

I took big gulps of oxygen; no matter how deeply I inhaled, my blood never felt fully saturated with it. Sir Walter's face became mottled with black and blue splotches. His upper lip curled back. As it curled, his yellow canines grew longer. When the sense of being lofted up high stopped, I placed a blanket over his head, gathered it in my arms, and stumbled down to Dad's secret room and deposited it there. Afterwards, I mopped up the blood with a towel. Because I had to keep stopping to take deep breaths, it took me an absurdly long time to perform these tasks.

Now that it had quit snowing, I needed to get outside and evaluate the situation. The highest windowpanes were snow-free; I could shatter them and break the grilles and, if I was careful, squeeze between the snow line and the head jamb. My flashlight was the readiest object. The sharp glass clinked to the floor. A few shards of nearly invisible glass clung to the frame, but I cleared them away before crawling through the gap and into the snow. The outside air proved thin as a blade.

I tried multiple times to stand up but couldn't manage it. I slithered through the snow toward the hemlock tree rising from the white powder. Finally I made it to the tree's multi-tiered framework and entangled myself in its labyrinth of branches. I crawled up, slowly, achingly. From the treetop I could get a view of the surrounding area.

Stars glimmered through the needles; their lights danced. Branches dumped snow with each step I took up the tree ladder. I labored towards the top, which I eventually reached, wavering on the conical crown, the tiny evergreen leaves tickling me like centipede legs.

Beyond the hemlock tree, my yard ended; Amelia's World had broken away. Far below, the earth curved. My house sat atop a pillar of snow like photographs I've seen of skyscrapers. Snow tapered into the distance, towards the earth's distant surface. I had been lifted into the heavens. Very few things were beyond belief anymore. I was no longer afraid, however, not even in these unheard-of circumstances. I'd overcome myself.

I turned to my house. I glimpsed its snow-laden roof along with the roof of Dad's workshop; the latter had come along for the ride. It stood on the other side of the house on the snow cliff's edge.

The distant mountains hundreds of thousands of feet below were crumpled like tinfoil. The sight confused me; I saw other landscapes that didn't look like Appalachia. Within a precisely hexagonal shape, the landscape, my landscape, was silver-white with snow as it should be. Yet beyond, in other hexagons, multiplying as far as the eye could see and adjacent to one another like vast honeycombs, were other landscapes, curving along the earth. One hexagon contained a green world, another a desert world, a third a night world, and yet another a flashing metal world.

Had the shimmering barrier blocked my entrance into these other worlds, where people like the woman on horseback roamed? It was as if an artist had carefully cut up the earth's landscapes and reshuffled them. Below was North Carolina, but that hexagon there could be a fragment of Russia, and that one Tokyo, for all I knew.

I lifted my arms. The links in my spine separated a little, elongated. I floated upwards. The camera floated up in front of my face and I caught the strap. I'd entirely forgotten I had it around my neck.

The moon crept around the earth and approached me as I hovered a few inches above the hemlock tree. But maybe it wasn't the moon. I hadn't seen the moon in so long. Was it the sun?

Yes and no—it was the harvest sun, the strange object I'd been seeing in the sky all along, sun and moon in one. I saw the object different ways. Upon one blink it was a silver moon. On another the golden sun. It was like flipping through different slides in a viewfinder. Then, as the orb hovered nearer to me, floating above the treetop, the two celestial objects ceased to appear distinctly, but existed as a single entity. I blinked and the same image remained: a golden, cratered orb that did not hurt my eyes.

The orb, the marriage of sun and moon, unveiled its full spherical beauty, a pearl in the darkness of outer space, rounding the earth and mushrooming to its true incomprehensible size like a fist of god.

I was drawn away from the treetop by the harvest sun's gravity, and as I flew towards it, I looked back. I could see that yes, a column of snow, a towering white monolith, had indeed lifted a piece of Amelia's World into outer space. I worried that the harvest sun would melt the snow and my house would drop, with my memories and Dad's photographs and Sir Walter's corpse, to shatter on a mountaintop.

I sailed towards the harvest sun. I breathed purely on the inside now, another pair of lungs working their bellows and flooding me with vitality. I imagined myself inside an umbilical cord that protected me from the annihilating power of outer space. Once or twice my arms swelled, and I feared they'd pop, but then they went back to normal.

The harvest sun and I met; it did not shatter me into toothpicks but shuddered to a halt in its orbit. I touched down on its sand. Glittering cliffs arced in an accordion's shape around me and two figures.

A woman in a nun's white wimple, black veil, and brown habit stood next to a white monkey in a cage, ensconced beside her in the golden sand. The monkey huddled. I did not recognize the woman's face. Her skin was luminous and layered like shining mica, the colors elusive. Her eyes were very close together and encroached on the bridge of her nose. She captivated but was neither beautiful nor ugly. And I'd never seen a monkey before except in photographs, and I'd certainly never seen one so near-transparent, so withered and sickly in its cage.

I stepped towards the two figures. The harvest sun emitted no cold, no heat. I turned back once again and glimpsed the white pillar rising from the earth; my house still capped it like a chimney pot.

The monkey in the cage, silent, unmoving, nevertheless sparked a yearning that I couldn't place. I peered through the wires and fixed my attention on the monkey's face. My soul stood still. For it wasn't a monkey at all, but the shriveled, wizened, naked body of Dad, like a man two hundred years old, covered with unnatural white hair below the neck. His face wasn't entirely obliterated by age and his characteristic attributes remained: the two straight wrinkles down his mouth, making his jaw resemble a ventriloquist dummy's; the five deep horizontal wrinkles across his forehead; wrinkles cross-stitching his neck; his jade eyes; the well-groomed nostrils and ears; and a light mustache fuzzing his upper lip as though it were any old evening. I'd found him at last, passed through the gauntlet to the harvest sun. He'd beckoned me here, after all.

I bent down to fling open the cage's door. I couldn't find one, however, and the woman in nun's habit intercepted my attempt, not through words but by bursting into flames. Her headdress and mantle showered into embers, floating behind her like banners. She stood before me stark naked. Even though my heart cried out to Dad, no mortal could ignore that sublime woman, terrible in both her remoteness and power. Black ringlets cascaded down her shoulders. Her left breast was missing.

Her other breast was plump and shot out wires of milk that branched into a net, a white lacework, which I now realized formed the walls of the cage in which my wizened little dad crouched. The Madonna of Carolina, in all her glory, had unveiled herself before me as Dad's jailer. There could be no mistake.

The Madonna observed me with tiger eyes. The wires of milk shooting from her right nipple lengthened and shortened, controlled as a spider controls its threads; the cage of breastmilk holding Dad contracted around him and loosened accordingly. His expression betrayed no recognition of me. He had the harried, vacant look of an Alzheimer's patient. How could I break through to him? Could I destroy this prison where he roosted and take him back to earth?

What had I to offer the Madonna? I patted my jeans—the figurine was gone, of course. Hopelessly I thrust my hands inside my pockets. Nothing was in there except a handful of mica. Where had I picked up these mica flakes? In my yard? At Icecandle Mountain? By the Chattooga? I remembered then that these were the remnants of the singing mica children. I offered their silvery-brown ashes to the Madonna, holding them aloft so that they shimmered.

The Madonna nodded. Her curls bounced and her tiger eyes softened. She inhaled deeply, voluptuously, creating the only current of wind in that windless landscape; the mica flew from my fingers like tiny insects, faster than thought, into her open mouth. She wolfed them down as though she were well accustomed to mica children and relished their mineral composition.

She smiled and spoke a silent word. My heart squeezed. It ran through me in a bolt of lightning. She said it again. I could not understand it. She shrugged her shoulders and examined the golden rocks around us that swelled like bales of honey-colored wheat in a Dutch Renaissance painting. She looked up and smiled again, as if arriving at an idea, and blushed darkly.

I glanced at Dad. He looked frightened and huddled into a tighter ball.

Like the television Sir Walter and I had watched glow and flicker in the storefront in Attic Window, and the luminous cloud that had risen out of Dad's stomach when he died, the Madonna's belly suddenly glowed with a rich blue light, an almost edible color, a thick acrylic of lapis lazuli. Something wriggled and heaved inside it, a living bread rising, leavening. A creature pressed a roving eye to her belly button. Red veins branched across her stomach. A tear widened and a squirming form toppled to the ground.

It had a glittering horn and a horse's face; its legs buckled like a newborn foal's. It was a unicorn foal, but its eyes, like those of the bear I'd seen in the shadowland, had a human expressiveness—even more than that bear, a familiarity that I responded to, recognized in my heart of hearts: it was a little chestnut unicorn that resembled Elodie almost to a T. Yet there was something more—something of me in it. My aquiline nose, my droopy lips. Was this the ultimate manipulation? Was this some semblance of our imaginary child in the guise of a unicorn?

The Madonna spat on her deflating belly. The vertical cesarean wound closed to a crystal scar.

A furry Elodie face had been stretched over the unicorn's elongated skull. The mane, just like Elodie's hair, was black, and the eyes blue-golden. But other qualities—her nose, lips, and posture—were mine. At the same time, she wasn't us. She was an addition, a subtraction. She was the impossible baby girl

Elodie and I would have had in a dream world where things turned out right.

Just a little unicorn foal. I gathered her sticky body in my arms. Air blasted from her nostrils. She blinked, made a sucking noise, and licked my shirt. She sneezed wet lunar dust, which floated across my face.

Dad shivered in his cage, feeling a cold I could not feel, or perhaps fear. Still he showed no recognition of me. I'd get him to remember, I said to myself, whenever this is over and I take him home.

"Tell me a funny story," the unicorn foal said with the voice of a human child, a girl's of about eight years old.

The creature's lips rooted at my shirt, and nibbled at my breast, but I pushed its muzzle away. Her horn scratched across my neck. The way the horn bobbed around like a knife made me uneasy.

"Come on, tell me a story. With details. Don't leave anything out, not even the smallest thing."

It was intoxicating to have a baby unicorn in my arms, its entire attention focused on me, breeding warm love. I had never wanted children, but it was a pleasure, now and then, to hold someone else's. I had never desired to wear the heavy mantle of a mother.

"I don't think I know any funny stories," I said. "And stop biting at my breast. I'm not your mamma. I don't have any milk. Maybe the Madonna does. Maybe she'll let Dad go and use her milk for something righteous, instead of keeping him, an elderly man, trapped in a cage."

The Madonna didn't alter her expression in the slightest.

"Please," the unicorn foal said. "Please please pretty please, just one story."

"Will you tell me one afterwards?"

"I'll try."

"Okay," I said. "Just promise not to chew on my breast anymore. Your teeth are long and sharp and hurt me. I don't have any milk in these withered old dugs. So promise."

"Promise."

"Well, let me see. I could tell a story about a woman that looks like you, a human woman I once loved, but I'm tired of that story. I've told it to myself too many times; I've also told too many stories about Dad, who is over there in a cage made of the Madonna's breastmilk; do you see him?"

The unicorn nodded.

"Would you think it funny if I told you that that good, sweet man, might have taken photographs of my lover's breasts, who looked a lot like you—that he took those photographs in secret, without my permission, and never confessed it to me? Though it's clear he confessed many things to the Madonna. But at the end of the day, that might be a story I made up. When I think about it I laugh; all these recent events are starting to seem funny. But I won't get into all that."

"None of that's very funny. Think of another story. I bet you have lots."

"Be careful with that horn and I'll try, okay?"

"Okay."

I focused on a golden canyon behind the Madonna and Dad. I brainstormed. I had so few funny stories from my life. Humor wasn't really in my disposition. Dad's friends often remarked how seldom I laughed. Some grew tiresome attempting to tell jokes about turkeys drunk on mash and the like, but at best they got a small chuckle out of me. While a face in an apple tree, mica children, a doppelgänger, a dancing bear, and a writer from the past stuck in my chimney all tickled me as I reflected on them, sitting in front of the Madonna in this alchemical landscape, a unicorn with a familiar face in my arms, I decided that another kind of story would be best.

"Once, not very long ago, I saw a woman on horseback, confident, silent, elusive. A woman of the tundra. I could not go to her because there was a wall of…let's say crystal, between us."

"Where did the wall come from?" the unicorn foal asked. "Are you sure that's what it was?"

Her eyes narrowed in a way that Elodie's would have. I tried not to get distracted.

"Now don't interrupt. That's rude. As I was saying, this woman rode a horse. Silver bells hung from its mane that tinkled sweetly. But she rode off into the unknown, and after waving to me for a moment, vanished into the hills. This woman, you might say, is a character. Someone that fascinates you and that you want to know. Well, this isn't a story about that woman, exactly, but a story of my search for her, which, if I'm lucky, might take place someday. And it's funny, or maybe droll is a better word—that means curious and amusing. But that's the best that I can do since you asked a person without much humor to tell a funny story. If you don't stop waving that horn around, I'll set you on the ground and send you back to that grand lady over there, who doesn't, from the looks of it, want anything to do with you. So there. Good.

"So imagine me, this old woman, a hermit and housebound most of her life, breaking through the crystal wall— don't ask me how—and going on an adventure to find this woman on horseback, riding, for all I know, into another world. Imagine me becoming a knight. Do you know what that is? Of course you do. You're smart for your age. But I won't become just any knight. I will make a suit of armor for myself. Not out of metal. I'd have no idea how to make that. This armor would be made out of the heads of dolls; hundreds of dolls' heads that I'd dig up from Dad's grave, nail together, and chink with clay. I'd whittle a spear out of hemlock, a witch's wood, with the skull of a once-famous writer that nobody reads anymore serving as the hilt. That spear would be my standard. I'd seek a horse to bear me into the unknown, to find the woman that fascinates me, to become a character like her, but maybe even greater, that others will tell about for a generation. Old Amelia with her armor of dolls' heads and her skull spear frightening children—if there are any children left—and becoming someone to read about in a fairy tale. Not a mother, not a jester, not good or evil, but a rider searching for a woman on horseback as King Arthur and his knights searched for the Holy Grail. And when I find her and hear the silver bells tinkling in the trees, I'll woo her, or win her horse, and maybe, if the fancy strikes me, take her captive.

"Think of me wearing an armor of dolls' heads and taking a woman captive."

"Wait. Is that the end of the story?"

"Yes."

"That's not very funny."

"I told you not to expect much."

"But still…I want another."

"No."

"Aww, come on."

"Absolutely not. We're done. Unless you want to tell me a funny story."

"But I can't think of any."

"Well, that's that, then."

I put the unicorn down in the golden dust. She rolled around and her hair glittered. She frolicked. She butted me with her muzzle and thrust out her pink tongue, curling it up and down.

"I have business with that lady," I said. "I can't amuse you anymore. I'm sorry. You're a distraction she has made."

"I'm thirsty."

"I'm sorry."

"I bet you have milk. Give me that breast."

"I don't. And I won't."

The unicorn foal hesitated. "Will you be my mommy?"

"I can't."

Dad was looking my way now. What a chance it would be to speak with him, or even an afterimage of him, beyond death. Who gets such an opportunity? So many pine away dreaming of it.

I stepped around the foal and approached the Madonna and Dad; they had somehow retreated from me while I was distracted. The foal nipped at my shin. It was both hard and easy to walk in the sand. It poured into my shoes. I had to extirpate my feet from its suction; whenever I did, I floated up and bounced a little, but the gravity created by the Madonna weighed me back down.

I knew what I had to say to her and it didn't come out faltering, because I felt confident and whole.

"I need you to give me Dad. He prayed to you. He worshipped you in the end. But his worship was such a small part of himself. I don't know if your ladyship gave me that figurine of the Virgin, or he did, or both of you did. You wanted me to come here. So I've come. But I can't offer you my devotion. While I didn't know all of Dad's secrets, and hold the keys to his inner life, I know for a fact I knew him better than you; sometimes knowing the exterior in all its richness is just as miraculous as knowing what's within. You were nothing more than a need born of his fear of death; you were the object of his desperation. My being here is proof that he loved what's on earth more: a few books and photography and purple martins and the mountains and breasts in all their lovely and idiosyncratic shapes and me, his only daughter. In the years he was

160

most himself, he loved earth's transient beauty more than anything else. The final chapters were a swift decay."

The Madonna tried to speak but it sounded like she was underwater. She looked scared.

"You're a just god like your son was just. Go and live as you will. You can't help Dad anymore."

By now I was so close to the Madonna I could kiss her. And part of me wanted to. She was sublime, devastatingly so. Her breath was manna, an azure field with the wheat blowing.

The Virgin wept as if her dead son once again lay in her arms, just taken down from the cross. The tears turned white. Her cheeks streamed with milk. I knew then that she'd forgive me, no matter what I did to her. No matter how perverse the means. She was so magnanimous. At last I had come to terms with the small violences within me. Sir Walter's last request had helped me with that.

I touched the cord of milk delicately. Just this little touch pricked my already-hurt fingertip.

The unicorn foal rasped behind me. Her heaves sounded dry, dehydrated, agonized.

I ducked under the cord of milk. The Madonna took her thin graceful finger and traced a circle around her breast. I remembered the painting I'd seen in the bookstore in Attic Window, in which the Virgin squeezed her nipple and the milk shot into the open mouth of the tonsured monk. I touched her breast. The flesh didn't give like I expected it to. I tapped on it; a hollow echo ran back and forth inside it. This breast was sick, like skin on the verge of molting and invaded with rot.

I took a bite of her breast. It tasted like the warm crust of bread with a layer of fibers adhering to the inside. These fibers melted in my mouth. I gnawed, carefully, around her breast's circumference, and she let me—and indeed, despite herself, glowed with pleasure; her back arched.

Whenever I bit, and the shimmering crust caved, my teeth intruded into a hollow space. Her fingernails dug into my arm. It was not a bloody affair as with Sir Walter's head. It was clean.

When I took the last bite of the Madonna's breast, and it fell into my hand, Dad's cage evaporated. He looked around confusedly, and saw me, really saw me. I could see an idea dawning on him. And one dawned on me, too. I needed to know something before dealing with Dad and going through the emotional toll, the ecstasy and pure wonder, of our reunion. I held the Madonna's breast to my eye and gazed through the darkness into the nipple's lens. Just as I had fancied, it acted as a telescope, marvelously sharp. Through it, I observed the pale blue earth.

Within each of the honeycomb cells I'd seen earlier—running like hexagonal tiles across the earth, each one maybe twenty miles across—there was a woman. I could see enough of their shapes and motions to know that they could only be women. Beyond my fragment of North Carolina, in, perhaps, Siberia and Japan and Antarctica and Kenya and a thousand landscapes I'd dreamed of but never imagined seeing, women of all ages roamed, some on horseback, others on foot. They busied themselves like bees in their cells. Thousands of women, and as I shifted the breast this way and that, the shimmering barriers, the hexagonal structures, seemed to spark and catch fire and dissolve, leaving burn marks on the snow and in the forests and across the cities.

If the barriers enclosing Hemlock Cove and Attic Window had dissolved, what had done it? Was it my severing of the Madonna's breast? Did it contain the power to divide me from the world?

After I finished peering through the nipple's lens, I threw her breast onto the golden sand, by the heaving unicorn foal, whose bones now bulged, whose skin had colloped in folds along her neck and who'd grown thinner. The unicorn foal latched her mouth onto the Virgin's nipple and sucked greedily, and maybe extracted a drop or two of milk. The foal shot me a look of accusation; her lips bled as from tiny shards of glass. She tried to stand up, but her four knees buckled.

"Lady," I said to the Madonna. "Can you save her? I can't carry her. I can't nurse her."

I gestured at the haggard unicorn.

The Madonna shook her head. She pointed at Dad, as though to say *only he can live*. She then pointed at herself, indicating she was to blame, that she'd bear the guilt of this act on her shoulders.

I bent down and picked up Dad. He weighed about as much as a two-year-old child.

He cleared his throat, squinted through glaucous eyes, and said, in a cackling, ghastly, blasted voice, "Melia?"

"I'm taking you home. All is not lost."

He fondled the Polaroid camera around my neck.

"*Hab' ich einen Fehler gemacht?*"

I had to ponder that for a moment.

"Yes, I think you made a mistake. Maybe it was just an error of the stars, but I'm with you now. That's all that matters. I love you. I wasn't always the best daughter. I know you worried about me. I know you had regrets, obsessions, and secrets. None of that matters right now. I'll ask questions later. I thank the Madonna for preserving you."

I got on my knees, which was tricky with Dad in my arms, and bowed to the Madonna.

The unicorn gasped and coughed in the sand. She thrust out her tongue and cast a wild eye at me.

I tried not to look at the foal. I stepped over her. I turned back to the Madonna, to make sure she hadn't had a change of heart and intended to stop us. She raised her hand in farewell and held it there.

Suddenly I recalled the two photos I had left in the camera. I lifted the Polaroid's viewfinder to my eye and snapped one of the breastless Madonna, a hand raised in farewell among the golden canyons. The undeveloped photograph spat out blue and splotchy. I pocketed it immediately, in the place the Virgin's figurine had once lived. I wanted a memento or a replacement.

The unicorn foal lay still, then one of her legs kicked, probably for the last time. I snapped one of her, too, and pocketed it, as perverse as that sounds. I couldn't load myself down with this child. My breasts were of no more use than the Madonna's. And the foal was the Madonna's own offspring and waif. I tossed the camera to the ground, my votive offering to the unicorn's brief life.

I shifted Dad to the piggyback position, kicked off, and we floated upwards.

In no time we reached the shores of our house on the pillar of snow. We tumbled into a drift.

I looked back and the harvest sun quivered and split into a kind of Venn diagram, with two overlapping circles that struggled to separate, to disentangle themselves from a common space; they then shot apart into separate entities: the old sun and the old moon. The sun snapped into its position far away and the silver moon raced around the other side of earth and hid behind it.

The Madonna of Carolina, with the dead unicorn in tow, darted like a white arrow into the distant reaches of the solar system. Her flight brought to my mind Simon Magis flying in the forum before the eyes of St. Peter; it appeared rapturous, as if she'd been released from a tremendous burden.

I tugged Dad's furry hand to get him to move. A bone dislocated, and he cried out, but it shifted back into place. I had to be delicate with him. I used all my remaining energy rolling that dear sack of bones across the snow to the window and guiding his body through the aperture and into the bright, sunlit living room. We curled up in a quilt, cuddling, just like I loved to do when I was a girl and crawled into bed with Dad and he sang me to sleep. His papery skin flaked on my clothes. My last thought before falling into a deep sleep was that this pillar of snow would melt now that the sun had returned to a state of self-sufficiency or that we'd suffocate and explode, unprotected in outer space.

The Wanderer

A heavy, dreamless sleep locked me in its tomb for a long, long time. When I woke after weeks, or months, or years, I still held Dad's infrequently breathing body, his skin flaking like wood chips. I listened to his heart. It thumped, paused, thumped twice, and paused for a spell before thumping again. I kissed his ear and he snored loudly, piggishly. I laughed. The walls of our house dripped with water, scrolls of wallpaper bowing towards the floor and paint trickling. The photographs on the walls—George Takeshi's "Unaka Peak" and Mossie Reynard's "Peach Harvest"—oozed and bubbled up, the migrating ink making the subjects almost indiscernible.

Breaches in the walls revealed a landscape of dripping branches, melting snow, and foaming freshets. Three diagonal tears in the ceiling, like claw marks, allowed shafts of yellow and green leaf-tinted light to slant and pool on the carpet. It was as if a tornado had hit our house.

I shook Dad. I shook him again. My heart skipped a beat. I yelled in his ear, shook him a third time, and he stirred. His open jade-eyed face smiled at me. He lifted a near-translucent monkey paw to my cheek and stroked it. His fingernails were yellow and very long.

"We've been sleeping a long time," I said.

He wiped a gunky line of sleep-seeds from his eyes. I did the same. We held out our fingers covered in the sleep-seeds and laughed at the grossness of it. I hadn't wiped off so much in my life.

"I never thought this moment would come," I said. "I never really, truly believed that I would see you again—never in my wildest dreams. Though something indestructible in me hoped."

166

I hugged Dad. I told him I loved him again and again as we lay there, together after a short separation that felt like years. Yet after the professions of love and apologies for my inadequacies, I couldn't help addressing a nagging question. I said as gently as I could, so as not to mortify him, "Dad, don't be angry. Don't be embarrassed. I don't care. You were my best friend and I've been so lucky. But I found the room in the closet under the dolls. And the pictures."

Dad's unnaturally white pallor, that seemed it could never hold color again, burst with red freckles.

"*Ich habe gewusst, dass du es finden wirst*," he rasped. "*Lass uns zusammen gehen...*"

It seemed he had forgotten how to speak English.

"Yes, let's go together. I'll carry you down there. Don't protest. I know you can't make it on your own."

My strength had returned somewhat, though I had to stop halfway and gulp down a glass of water—the pipes ran with it again, even though the house was riven open to the elements and in the first phase of total dissolution. I held the glass to Dad's lips and he spluttered out the water. He couldn't hold any down. That unnerved me but didn't necessarily surprise me. I used a butterknife to pry open the trapdoor in the closet and we descended the ladder with him riding me piggyback. By the time I touched the concrete I felt like I had hiked three miles. The sun blazed so brightly through the rooms above that, even down here, we could see duskily, as by candlelight. I flipped on the light switch. Sir Walter's head lay in a corner, covered with a brown-stained blanket. Dad grunted something referencing it, but I ignored him.

The photographs, unlike those upstairs, hadn't been damaged by our miraculous transport or fall or gradual, snow-buoyed descent from outer space. I didn't have the mental energy to piece together why we were alive, with the house surviving mostly intact. A last miracle of the Madonna, I suppose.

"*Die Jungfrau*," he said sadly. "*Ist sie weg?*"

"Yes, her ladyship is gone. Did these photographs have anything to do with her? In that Testimonial you wrote you mentioned seeing the Madonna above Devil's Courthouse—was she missing her breast? And when was that? Why didn't you ever tell me about these visions or photographs? You know I wouldn't have cared. I'm offended that you thought them secrets worth keeping. But what I really want to know—don't bother yourself with all those other questions now, I'm sorry, I know this is a lot and I see you struggling. Don't struggle. You're here with me. I love you. What I want to know is: did you take pictures, private pictures, of Elodie McWaters—the woman I loved?"

Questions rose from the depths of his bleary eyes. He nodded his head yes, shook it no.

I approached and pointed to the photograph in question: large breasts like the ones that had popped out of Elodie's nightgown when she raised her arms to heaven in a sudden exclamation.

Dad touched the photograph gingerly. He scratched its back. He tried to pull it off the wall, but he was so weak he couldn't even accomplish that. So I peeled it off for him. And on the back of the photograph was a date and a name. Why had I been so stupid not to look there?

"Imogene Bascom, 1921."

I recalled Imogene then, Dad's photographer friend, who'd bragged about how she'd taken portraits of William Butler Yeats and Lillian Gish. Her dress had always hung loosely over her chest; she would've been the right age for the breasts in the photograph. I realized I'd been wrong. They weren't

Elodie's. Dad, old quirky pervert that he was, would've never betrayed me like that.

I remembered the list of names that I'd found in the folder labeled "Cold Weather Scenes." It occurred to me that this list catalogued all the people whose chests he'd photographed over the years, clearly in places outside our property (I hadn't recognized any of the backgrounds—probably at people's homes, in Olto and Gallow Hollow, in Asheville and the mountains thereabout). I knew many of the names on the list: Dad's friends and various locals. It hurt a little to think of his life beyond me. I should have asked Dad more questions, insisted on being a bigger part of his life. But maybe he wouldn't have wanted that. Maybe our life together as it was had been as right and perfect as it ever could've been; maybe we needed some distance, some secrets, to love properly, as strange as that sounds. When I first found that list of names, I'd mentally noted that Elodie was not on it. Her husband was and so were her sisters and mother.

I held Dad and cried into his shriveled shoulder. He lifted his infant's mouth and kissed a cord in my neck.

"I would've laughed at you if I'd known about these photos. I wouldn't have minded a bit. I had my obsessions and quirks, too. If you hadn't found religion, we could've shared so much those last years."

He pressed his nose into my armpit. His words were raspy and soft, but I heard him whisper, "I was always afraid of your laughter."

On a beautiful spring day, I touched my forehead to the roots of the poplar tree under which Dad, my original Dad, was buried. I took a shovel and dug until its metal struck the coffin he'd built many years ago in preparation for his death, and kept in storage, upright against the back wall of the toolshed. I used a hammer's claw to pry it open and was greeted first by the smell of decay and mugwort, which I'd crushed and sprinkled on his remains. But when the lid was entirely off and put aside, a hundred dolls' faces gazed at me blankly. One by one I exhumed them and piled them on a pallet.

My original Dad lay there naked. He'd said long ago that he wanted to be buried without clothes, to go to the earth as any other creature would go. I avoided absorbing the details of his putrefying body. I looked forward to a time when I didn't have to record everything in my mind or on paper, notching every detail on my mental doorframe. I went inside the house and folded Dad's stiff, wasted, apish double into my arms. The Madonna's prisoner had died the night before.

I lowered my miniature father into the grave and laid him across Dad's stomach.

I resealed the coffin and pushed the dirt back into the hole. I brought the dolls, armful by armful, into the leaning, collapsing hovel that was once a sound and cozy home.

I became quite handy, repairing parts of the house that absolutely needed it in the short term, but mostly I was content to let it decay, to war with the elements and lose, to make it a home for turkey vultures, for the floors to warp and buckle and the furniture to erode and fray and unravel. The secret basement would fill with water. If the frogs came back, they'd spawn in it, and the photographic dyes would leak into the water and become part of the makeup of their tadpoles.

Just now a purple martin landed on the windowsill and then flew away.

Dad's workshop is nowhere to be found on the property, in Hemlock Cove or the surrounding mountains. I imagine it floating somewhere in outer space, the blue folders emptied of their contents, and thousands of photographs orbiting his workshop like the rings of Saturn.

A moment ago I smoked the last of the bright leaf tobacco and placed my corncob pipe in the fireplace with the stub of the Virgin Mary figurine. One day this chimney, with Sir Walter's skeleton inside it, will be all that's left of our house.

I am no longer a hermit; no longer a daughter in need of an anchor; no longer a bereaved woman or a heartbroken girl. I saw off the dolls' heads and make myself a suit of armor from them, an uncanny thing if ever there was one. It won't guard me from harm, made, as it is, of porcelain, cloth, wood, rubber, plastic, and papier-mâché; that's not the point. The heads of the two cornhusk dolls I stole from Dad when I was a young woman I'll wear like jewels atop my shoulder plates. With my white hair cascading upon those decapitated dolls' heads, and the smirk of a crone, and Sir Walter Scott's skull as the cross-guard of my lance of sharpened hemlock, I'll find a horse, elk, or bear and befriend it and ride it into unknown lands.

I have determined for certain, from the summit of Devil's Lozenge, that the shimmering walls enclosing me have collapsed. First I'll go to Bear Shadow City, and if I cannot find an animal friend there, I'll delve into the mountain caves seeking a beast to ease my passage and add to the formidability of my presence. I'll delve down to the rumored dragon at the earth's root if I must. The going will be slow, but after I find this animal friend, I can manage. If I encounter rivals, I will teach them the indignities of mercy. I will make a name that will pass through a hundred women's mouths for a generation. I will find the woman on horseback and demand a high toll. I will love her, and she will love me, or I will take her horse, and leave her, embracing the myths of this life.

I pull a Ziplock bag from my pocket and take out the two Polaroids: the one of the Madonna of Carolina waving farewell and the other of the unicorn minted with Elodie's and my features, half-buried in golden, alchemical sand. I won't burn them as some people burn photographs of those they'd rather forget. These proofs of my recent encounters with the sacred I'll carry through the rest of my allotted time on earth like a passport; unlike the photographs of Elodie and me, I will keep them with me always. Once I heard that a famous writer, I can't remember who, maybe a Swedish one, kept a photograph of his playwright rival above his desk so he could always gaze upon it, and breathe in the fires of hate and inspiration. Perhaps, on the journey outside my Appalachian honey cell that I've been busy circling for seventy-one years, I'll take them out from time to time to remind me of who I am in foreign lands, and who I am not, to keep my heart honest as a little child's. There may be no wisdom in travel and adventure, and much boredom, but I will experience love, hate, and suffering, like fresh-cut roots, before I die.

It is time to end this journal, grown into a book, and write an epigraph. On second thought, no—Sir Walter would do that. And this account was written for no man, but as a prayer to the fires of decreation.

I scribble these final lines in the orchard. I've returned to this place, where it all started, as though it were the center of the labyrinth all along. The branches are bare but the apple heaps are here. They'll always be here. After my last word is written, I will place this spiral notebook, whose cover is an illustration of a foxfire fungus glowing at night, atop an apple heap. The ink will blur in the rain, and the soggy and disintegrating paper will melt like a brief mist on the mountains.

Maybe one of the strong-minded and secret women, one of the few who are left, will find my journal and read it, but I don't expect or even want that. I'd prefer this small part of me to belong to the run of apples and flesh of Appalachia.